AMERICAN

Z

BLOODLINEZ

J.G. FLETCHER

Copyright © 2018 by J.G. Fletcher

Published by
TSOMBIE Inc.
A Phase III Publishing Company
Clarksville, Tennessee
https://tsombie.com
https://jg-fletcher.com

ISBN: 978-0-9997096-1-0

eBook ISBN: 978-0-9997096-0-3

Library of Congress Control Number: 2018902688

Clint, Stephanie, Tim,

Thank you for the support and motivation

ONE

It's over, Mike Hardy thinks to himself. My life is over. I am never going to lead The Society. I am never going to lead the new America. I am never going to lead, anything, ever. The chance of living the life I always wanted is now gone. Tasha is going to take the throne and I am going to be her slave, serving under her for the rest of my life. The Hardy dynasty is over.

Mike stares at the engraved plaque on the back wall of the conference room.

Imagine the greatness people can achieve if someone forces their hand.

The motto of The Society.

He reads the motto, over and over again, and thinks about all of his recent failures. And he thinks about how easy it all would be if he was just one of them, a TSOMBIE. Never knowing your failures in life. Never dealing with disappointment. There is a certain peace there, he thinks to himself.

Being an immune bloodline carried with it a harder burden, knowing.

Mike shifts his eyes back down to the table. He looks at Tasha again. He stares at her, sitting there so calm and snug, knowing she now has total control of the reigns at AGI. She would most certainly be named an official successor of The Society in the distant future.

Mike looks at his watch. Nine o'clock.

He looks around the conference room at everyone, again with disdain. All twenty-three original bloodlines were board members. They maintained the critical positions within The Society. But they only accounted for about a quarter of all eighty-eight board members worldwide, which were always present for these monthly and quarterly meetings, in person or via live video and telephone.

Mike looks at his watch again. Ten minutes after nine o'clock. Ten minutes after the meeting was supposed to start. Then the doors open, and everyone sitting at the conference table stands up.

"Good morning everyone. Please, take your seats." Mr. Hardy motions for his assistant to take his coat and he begins to take his seat at the head of the large table.

Mike sits back down after his father barely glances at him, appearing to avoid even acknowledging his presence now.

Mr. Hardy opens a folder in front of him. He takes a drink of water and scans through the folder, reading the files. Everyone sits in silence, waiting. After a few moments he places the folder down and looks around the room at everyone, finally focusing in on the large projector screen.

"Okay, let's begin. I will save my comments for the end." Mr. Hardy looks to Tasha.

Tasha nods. She smiles at Mike for a fraction of a second before she begins briefing. It is very slight, but Mike notices the brief display of arrogance.

She clicks a button on the remote to move forward to the next slide.

The new slide that appears is an image, an overview of the world map. All countries are color coded with percentage numbers over them.

The board members study the slide for a moment in silence.

All the countries are green, '95%' or above Phase Three complete. There are a few areas and individual states within some of the previously foreign countries that are amber, between '90%' to '94%' Phase Three complete.

"As everyone can clearly see on the map, all of our Society countries are green for being Phase Three complete and have no major issues. There are still a handful of underdeveloped civilian populations in Asia, India, and Africa, that remain amber due to being so secluded. However, all of our regional Society leaders in those areas have confirmed that there are no concerns. There is also a slight time delay in these areas, due to previous Phases being administered later than everywhere else. And, less than one percent of these indigenous populations are believed to have not received any vaccinations at all yet. After these isolated populations are Phase Three complete, they will be relocated and repurposed in other regions, as test subjects or factory workers."

Tasha clicks the remote again and changes the slide.

"Moving on. As of last week, the CIA, FBI, all branches of the military and government, including the previous foreign nation equivalents, have all been confirmed one hundred percent Phase Three complete. This includes what was previously known as North Korea. However, we are still in the process of relocating those populations south of Seoul and converting the land in the north into the approved Society resorts and vacation areas. And for everyone in the room and on the net, there are still three resorts and two million acres still open for bids. Back to topic, the military TSOMBIEs will be used for implementing the remaining Phase Three injections in the isolated areas we discussed earlier. The military will also be utilized to transport and relocate those populations, after they are confirmed Phase Three."

Tasha places the remote down on the table.

"The last thing that I will discuss before I turn it over to Mr. Scott Barnes, is the remaining civilian population right here in old America that are not Phase Three yet. We estimate that total to still be in the high hundreds, and possibly up to the low thousands. Our increase in targeting operations over the past few months alone has resulted in the successful capture, or kill, of over twelve-hundred uninfected. Excuse me, non-TSOMBIEs. The majority of these civilians were anti-vaccination group members. We found a small number of these personnel to be associated with the AGI and Society bombings that occurred over three months ago, after we implemented Phase Three worldwide. And all of the credit for our successful captures and kills goes to Scott and his team."

Tasha begins a small clap and everyone else joins in for a moment.

Mike looks to his left at Scott Barnes, sitting in the chair that he used to sit in.

There was really nothing for Mike to hate or dislike about the man, other than him taking over his job as the targeting and surveillance department executive. He was similar in age to Mike, good-looking, nice, and smart.

Mike didn't necessarily hate him, but he did hate the fact that he had been reduced to nothing more than an assistant in a department that he used to run. Mike knew his father had no choice but to demote him after the bombings.

Now though, looking at Scott Barnes standing there, it reminds Mike of all the responsibility he had lost. Now, all he can do is sit, and listen.

"Thank you, Tasha. Thank you." Scott stands and shakes Tasha's hand.

The clapping subsides, and the room quietens down again.

Scott begins briefing.

"Our primary targeting and surveillance is on the remaining, non-TSOMBIEs, and the few non-Society bloodlines that have not been captured yet. There are just nine, non-Society bloodline individuals remaining. Six are assumed to be right here in the old United States, with three of those being the Rawlings bloodline. Robert, Julia, and Justin. The other three in old America are not related, and they have not been sighted since around last year. We believe that they may be hiding within the anti-immunization groups, and that they have went off the grid and underground, so to speak. And, there are two siblings that remain in China that we are closing in on. And lastly, there is one loner in Germany that we are also close to finding, and it is really just a matter of time with him being by himself. The rest of the non-Society bloodlines, that we have captured, are being held in our secure 'community-like' camp, in Kentucky. They are currently still being screened and evaluated for possible Society integration and for reproductive purposes, to preserve immune bloodlines for our current members that have any medical limitations. Switching gears, we are also closing in on the Georgia, Tennessee, and Washington bombers. We know that Robert Rawlings was responsible for Nashville personally, but we still suspect he had help for the other states. However, as Ms. McNeil briefly mentioned earlier, we have successfully killed or captured almost every known contact of his that helped with the bombings."

Mike could feel the eyes of everyone staring at him as Scott continued discussing details about the bombings. Eyes casting blame on him. And he just sat there and took it, again.

"All repairs have been completed as of two weeks ago to all facilities that were damaged, due to the bombings. And as for the buildings that were no longer salvageable, operations were simply shifted to the nearest medical or university research facility, since we control everything now. The last topic I will discuss is the update on our newly implemented rapid scanners. As you all may have noticed, we have them installed pretty much everywhere now. Tollbooths, gas stations, all public and business buildings, and all public transport locations. We are also about fifty percent complete with having them installed in all residential homes. But, all Society members and mission essential TSOMBIEs have them in all of their homes. Pending any questions, that concludes my update."

Scott nods at Mr. Hardy and takes his seat.

"Thanks, Scott. Okay. I know everyone is anxious about moving into our new operational headquarters along the old Pennsylvania Avenue. Construction will be complete in the next month or two, for all of the new security upgrades and department additions. I am also sure that everyone is aware of our upcoming Society leadership elections, and of the candidates that are running for election. First, is myself, being the primary candidate. And I am proud to announce the other two candidates, recently nominated by the board. Mr. Walter Rockmann, the primary financier and contributor to TSOMBIE research funding. And General Tristan 'Trip' James, recently appointed to the new position of American Global Armed Forces Commander."

There is a brief outburst of clapping from around the room as the announced candidates all stand and smile. The room quietens down, and the candidates take their seats after shaking a few hands.

Mr. Hardy and Tasha look at each other in a moment of angst, then Mr. Hardy forces himself to smile and addresses the room again.

"Voting will take place at our inaugural, Society Convention, which will be held on America's birthday this year. And that birthday of course being her new American birthday, the day that we began Phase Three and changed the world, forever!"

There is a loud and confident round of applause from around the room.

Mike could not help but to feel bad while listening to his father talk about the new election process, and about the candidates and voting.

The bombings and the failure to capture Rawlings brought a certain level of doubt, and lack of confidence, in the Hardy's ability to maintain power. Mike hated that he might be responsible for the end of the Hardy dynasty reign within The Society. After more than a century of the Hardy family being at the head of The Society, they now faced losing it. And it was all due to one man. One man's ambition. One man's drive to never stop. Robert Rawlings.

Mike forces himself to stop thinking about everything running through his mind and tunes back into the meeting as his father is finishing up.

"...And this will give us enough time to ensure that we have, without a doubt, one hundred percent Phase Three implementation, before we start the new communication message packages for the TSOMBIE public. And we want to rule out any chance of the non-TSOMBIEs receiving any of our new, truthful messages about The Society. Even though they number in a miniscule amount, there is no need for us to take any unnecessary risks with them. I don't think any of us want to deal with an uprising, no matter how small it is. Well, ladies and gentlemen, I think that covers everything I had to talk about. Pending any questions from around the room?"

"How much longer is it going to take to bring Rawlings and his remaining rebels to justice?" A board member asks from one of the overseas monitors. "It has been over three months now."

The man's face appears on the projector screen for everyone to see. It is the regional Society leader for Europe, Charles Walker, a known campaign supporter of Walter Rockmann.

A stir of quiet conversation begins around the table, as other members in the room shake their heads in concurrence with Mr. Walker's comment.

Mike watches silently as Tasha and his father look at each other with mild concern. Mike then looks at Mr. Rockmann, who is smiling in his chair at the opposite end of the table.

Scott Barnes leans over and whispers into Mr. Hardy's ear. Mr. Hardy shakes his head and addresses the, now somewhat noisy, conference room.

"Okay. Okay. Ladies and gentlemen, please." Mr. Hardy moves his right hand up and down, motioning for everyone to bring their conversations to an end. He waits a few seconds for the talking to stop.

"Now, I completely understand the concern to put an end to the Rawlings issue at hand. So, I can promise you this, I can assure you all that he is no longer a threat. And we are very close to dialing in on his exact location. It is only a matter of time now before he, they, are found and dealt with. With our security now doubled at AGI and Society facilities, and rapid scanners emplaced virtually everywhere, Rawlings and any of his few remaining followers pose no threat to us. Rest assured."

About half of the members in the room seem to accept Mr. Hardy's response. But the other half of the board members make a few more comments, quietly amongst themselves.

The microphones go mute on the television screens, with mouths still moving on the other end, clearly talking with other members at their various locations about his comments.

Avoiding any further questions, or topics of tension and conflict, Mr. Hardy decides to adjourn the meeting.

"Thank you everyone for your attendance today, and as always, for your continued support."

Everyone stands, following Mr. Hardy, and place their hands over their hearts for a few seconds in silence. Small conversations begin almost immediately afterwards around the room.

Mr. Hardy shakes hands with a few of the members near the doors on his way out, appearing as if he was fleeing the scene of a crime. Mike knew that he was trying to leave before getting cornered by anyone inquiring into areas of contention, areas that now seemed to be brought up more frequently at every meeting.

Mr. Hardy locks eyes with Mr. Rockmann at the other end of the room just before he exits. Mr.

Rockmann smiles at him, while shaking hands with a small crowd of Society members gathering around him. Mr. Hardy breaks eye contact and looks back at the table, in the direction of Tasha and Mike. He motions for them to follow him with his head.

Mike feels a rush of excitement for being invited to his father's office again after a meeting. Tasha rolls her eyes as she passes in front of Mike on the way out.

"Getting invited back into the old man's office, huh?" Scott asks Mike at the door.

Scott extends his hand to Mike and they shake. "I'll see you later, Mike."

Mike straightens his tie with a small sense of renewed confidence and follows behind his father and Tasha.

Mike closes the door to his father's office, as he is the last to enter, and walks toward an open chair in front of his father's desk.

"Mike, I need you to get our family jet and security detail ready to leave tonight. Your mother wants to go to Paris for the weekend."

"Yes, sir." Mike responds and begins to take his seat.

"Oh, umm, that will be all, Mike. That is all I needed from you. Please close the door on the way out."

Tasha almost laughs, but she quickly converts her reaction into a light cough.

"Yes, sir." Mike says softly.

"Thanks, Mike."

"And Mike, could you please have the secretary bring in some fresh coffee for us? Thanks." Tasha asks with an entitled tone in her voice.

Mike nods quietly and walks slowly out of the office. The brief feelings of confidence and excitement quickly fading away with each step he takes. Shame and embarrassment now re-staked claim to their throne in Mike's emotional kingdom. He can hear their conversations start as he exits, and he asks himself, is this what my life has been turned into? Scheduling flights and fetching coffee?

He turns and looks back at them as he closes the door, talking and laughing. He pauses at the secretary's desk and begins to open his mouth, but he stops himself.

"Get your own damn coffee," he says to himself and then walks away.

TWO

The bunker itself was somewhat comforting, but at the end of the day, it was still a bunker. Enough batteries to keep light sources on and use antiquated electronics. Enough exercise equipment to stay healthy. Somewhat fresh air, not too stale. The air filtration system was connected to a battery power source, controlled by an automatic timer. There were multiple tunnels and hallway corridors in the bunker. One hallway extension ran towards a small river, opposite direction of the cabin, and there was a room that contained several small generators for backup power sources, and to run a few higher-powered electronics. There were several rooms and bedrooms throughout the bunker. Some were small with only one mattress or cot, while other rooms were larger and contained several. A small, makeshift bathroom with the bare amenities resided in the back corner of the bunker, and there were a couple of single toilets spread throughout the bunker. There was a non-potable water source in the main bathroom, extending down from the metal ceiling and controlled by a valve on a pipe. The water had a lake-like smell to it, safe enough to use for personal hygiene but not really safe to drink. It all appeared to everyone as if Robert had really put in the time and effort on designing this bunker.

The past few months in the bunker had been relaxing and peaceful for everyone. A little crowded at times, but still peaceful. But now, they had arrived at the first 'stir-crazy' time in the bunker, and attitudes started to reflect in their conversations and demeanor.

* * *

"Joo-yah. Joo-yah."

Julia opens her eyes to little Samantha staring at her. Julia closes her eyes and pulls the cover over her head.

"Joo-yah. Joo-yah."

Julia waits a few seconds and then quickly throws the cover off. "Roarrr! I'm going to get you now you little munchkin. Roarrr!"

She grabs Samantha and pulls her onto the small mattress and begins tickling her.

Samantha laughs and then squirms away from Julia, running off into the other room.

Julia smiles and watches her run, awkwardly but fast. Julia catches a glimpse of Justin in the kitchen area as the large curtain door swooshes open from Samantha running out.

She stretches for a moment and then looks over into the small room beside her. She looks at Brian, sitting quietly in the far corner of the room, playing checkers by himself. She gets up and walks to his doorway.

"Hey, Brian. You want me to play a game with you?"

He just keeps moving the game pieces around without saying anything.

She lets out a deep breath and walks into the kitchen, where Justin is sitting down.

Justin looks up from the small electronic game he is playing as Julia walks in.

"Good afternoon." He says, as his thumbs continue plugging away at the game.

"Yeah, yeah." Julia fires back, as she pours a cup of coffee from the nearly empty pot.

She pulls her hair back from her face into a small ponytail, using the rubber band from her wrist.

Julia had let her hair grow longer again over the past several months. She had also stopped her daily routines and exercise regimen. She was relaxed now, surrounded by her family in the bunker, and she had settled in comfortably for the long haul. She was happy now, not stressed like her first tour in the bunker when she was all by herself.

Julia squirms from the initial bitter taste of the stale coffee as she takes a seat beside Justin at the table. She pours some water in the cup to cut the blackness of the thick coffee into a mild shade of brown.

"Come on, Justin. You let him make the coffee again?"

"Sorry. He beat me waking up. I don't think he ever slept."

Julia stretches her head to look at Robert in his operations room, at his computers, as usual.

"It is nice to have generators this time, to enjoy these little amenities. But man, his coffee is going to kill us before The Society ever gets a chance to." Julia says, smacking her lips from another drink.

Justin cracks a smile and then shrugs his shoulders at the game he's playing. "Come on man!"

"What level are you on now?"

"Ten."

"Still?"

"Yep."

Irritated, Justin turns off the game and starts making lunch.

Julia takes her coffee and walks into Robert's operations room.

Maps, pictures, and notes were on every wall. Two laptops were side by side on a small desk with several monitors. Julia, Justin, and Dave had all tried helping Robert, but they knew less about decryption than Robert did. They couldn't help. Now, Robert lived, breathed, and ate in the operations room, trying desperately to crack the encryption on the files Nichols had sent him before he died. Over three months of working on the computers had gone by, and Robert had only decrypted two files, what Nichols was able to decrypt in just a few hours.

Julia walks up to him, unnoticed due to his intense focus on the computers.

She feels sorry once again for not being able to help him.

"Dad." She gently places one hand on his shoulder, startling him.

"Hey, sweetie. Sorry, I've been locked in for the past few hours. I'm real close to figuring out this last line of code to open up another file."

"Justin said you didn't sleep last night, again."

"I'm okay. I'm catching a few minutes here and there. I just don't want the computers to freeze up again. I am really close here. Is that coffee I smell?"

Robert reaches over his shoulder and takes the cup from Julia. He takes a huge drink before she can say anything. He shakes his head and holds the cup under the desk lamp, observing the coffee coloration, light brown. He looks at Julia with a scowl on his face.

"How do you drink this watered-down stuff?"

They both smile, knowing they feel the same way about each other's coffee preference.

"I know, I know. I make it too strong for you amateurs."

"Why don't you take a break, Dad? And get something to eat? Justin is making lunch right now."

"Lunch? Man, I guess I really have been locked in here. Yeah, I'll be in there in a few minutes."

Julia reaches over his shoulder and grabs her cup.

"I'll take my, watered-down, amateur coffee back now."

They smile again, and Julia walks back to the kitchen area.

Julia sees Dave and Amy now sitting at the table, eating with Justin. Dave is letting Samantha eat from the table, sitting in his lap.

Julia takes a seat.

They all smile softly and continue eating, all thinking the same thing but not saying it.

Julia knows they are all getting stir-crazy.

Justin places a plate down for Julia, and then he adds one for Robert's empty spot. He looks around the corner at Robert, still at the computers. He stops eating and begins tapping his fork on his plate, breaking up the awkward silence. He leans forward into the group at the table and begins talking softly, almost whispering.

"How much longer are we going to sit around and do nothing? It has been over three months now, and Robert said the plan was to not initiate contact with anyone before the first ninety days. Well, it has been over ninety days. What is he waiting on?"

The group looks around at each other but doesn't respond to Justin.

"Look, I will say something to him, but I don't want to be by myself here."

Justin waits for a response, but again, there is just silence.

"Well, what do you guys think we should do then?"

Julia puts down her fork and is about to say something, but Robert's voice cuts her off before she has a chance to speak.

"What you should do about what, Justin?" Robert asks calmly, as he walks into the kitchen from around the corner. He walks to the coffee pot and starts making a fresh brew, with his back turned towards everyone.

They all look at each other, quietly voting. Then they look to Justin, silently giving him the okay to tell Robert what they were talking about.

"The plan, your plan, was to go blackout on communications with the other contacts for the first ninety days. Well, we have passed ninety days, and we have not contacted anyone yet, and you haven't even mentioned anything about it. You just stay locked away in your little hole, night and day, never asking for anyone to help. Meanwhile, we are all going crazy out here, Robert. We are just sitting around with our thumbs up our rear-ends."

Robert turns his head slightly, and then looks down at the floor, facing away from them still. He waits for the coffee to finish brewing, and they all sit quietly, waiting for his response.

He pours a cup of coffee. Then he tops it off with a splash of alcohol from the nearly empty bottle on the counter.

They all agreed to ration the alcohol and keep their consumption to just one bottle per month, for everyone to share. This was agreed upon to keep their heads clear, should they ever need to move quickly, at a moment's notice.

"We need to make another supply run to the cabin." Robert says, taking a small sip.

"Come on, Robert. I'm serious here. When are we going to start doing something? Anything?"

Robert takes another small sip and finally turns to face the group, all of them looking anxiously back at him.

"I know that I have been secluding you guys from helping me lately. And, I have not been talking with you all that much. And well, I'm sorry about that, I am. It was not intentional, I swear. I've just been so focused on decrypting these files lately…well, I guess I put everything else on the back burner. And I'm sorry. And you're right, Justin, it is time we reach out to the others and get an update."

Justin, and everyone else, smiles at the unexpected and conceding response from Robert.

"I promise to put a pause on the decryption after today, and then we will start initiating communications with the others tomorrow."

Robert smiles at Samantha eating, and then he smiles at the group.

"Sit down with us, Dad. You need to eat something and take a break."

Robert nods his head at Julia and takes a seat beside her.

"Another one of Justin's tasteful dishes I see." Robert coughs out, after he takes a bite of the canned meat and vegetable medley, smothered with hot sauce.

Dave, Amy, and Julia all laugh softly.

Justin looks at them with a strong and serious glare. He holds it for a few seconds and then lets it go and starts laughing with them.

"So, what have you guys been up to lately?" Robert smiles at the group.

They eat lunch and continue with much needed casual conversation with Robert, changing topics frequently.

Robert's interaction dilutes everyone's anxiety, and they all relax. The feeling of being 'cooped-up' fades away, for the time being.

THREE

Mike closes several open files at his desk, preparing to go home for the day.

He stops for a moment and looks around at the Phase Three analysts that he was now surrounded by every day. His desk was now in the middle of the targeting and surveillance department, no office anymore.

Mike enters a slight daze as he watches the TSOMBIE employees from his shift, all of them preparing to go home, same as him. The only difference being, Mike was conscious of the hell he was living in.

Then he looks at Scott, sitting in what used to be his office.

His former assistant, Chris Trendell, passes by his desk on the way to Scott's office, waking him out of his semi-frozen state.

Mike continues closing out his files and then leaves his desk.

Scott looks up from the end of day brief he is receiving from his assistant and waves to Mike. Mike waves back as he walks by the glass windows.

There were no hard feelings between the two of them, they were both simply following orders and doing the jobs they had been given, doing what was best for them, and what was best for The Society.

* * *

Mike sticks his hand into the new rapid scanner at the entrance of his gated home.

"Kids, your father is home."

Mike's wife stands in the doorway, waiting for him to come inside.

Mike gives his wife a kiss as he enters the large home.

"Hi, sweetheart. So, how was your day? How did the meeting go?" Melissa says, taking the briefcase from him.

Mike just looks at her with discouraging eyes.

She gives him a quick hug.

"That bad? Don't worry about it, Mike. And look on the bright side, you get to keep coming home at normal hours and spending more time with us."

She lets go and looks at him.

Mike looks back at her, still upset.

"The past couple of months have been wonderful having you here all the time, and not having to see you work yourself to death. The boys have their father back. You and I don't fight any more like we used to. We actually 'talk' to each other, regularly. It has been great, hasn't it?"

Mike's scowl fades and he begins to smile. "It has been great honey. You're right, I shouldn't worry so much."

"Dad!"

Their youngest son runs into the living room and jumps into Mike's arms.

"Hey buddy. Where's your brother at?"

"Watch out Dad! Let Zack go!" Says the oldest son, Jack. He then aims a laser gun toy at Mike and his brother, pulling the trigger repeatedly.

Zack jumps down from Mike's arms and takes off running up the stairs.

"I got you Zack!"

"You did not!"

Mike and Melissa laugh at their children playing, and they hug each other.

"See, all of us are so happy to have you home all the time now." Melissa says.

They hug each other for a few more seconds, and then she takes a step back.

"I hate to change the subject, but your mom called today. She wanted to tell me that she is going to Paris for the weekend."

"Yeah, I know. I had to get the plane and security team ready for her."

"Well, then she asked me to go with her."

"Really? What did you tell her?"

"I told her no, of course. I told her we already had plans."

"Plans?"

"Yes, plans. Don't worry, you'll see later tonight."

Mike smiles as Melissa slowly backs away from him and walks up the stairs.

"And I sent the maids and other staff home for the weekend, so it's just us here."

He hears her voice trailing off as she disappears into the mansion-like home, "Boys, be careful and don't play too…"

Mike walks into his study room and pours himself a small cocktail. He takes a seat and turns on his computer. He pauses in the middle of logging on to check his email. He pauses and thinks. He thinks about everything his wife had just said.

"The hell with it," he says to himself, smiling.

Mike makes a vow to himself as he takes a small drink, I am not going to think about work at all this weekend. I am going to relax and enjoy it.

He turns off the computer and then his cell phone. He closes the door to his study and walks up the stairs, smiling with every step. Smiling at the thought of forgetting about work. Smiling at the thought of forgetting about Tasha and his father. And smiling at the thought of forgetting about The Society.

FOUR

"Ms. McNeil, Mr. Barnes is here to see you."

Scott stands beside Tasha's assistant in the doorway, "I have an update for you on the Han siblings."

Tasha motions for Scott to come inside her office and have a seat.

"Okay, yes, I'll have to get back with you on that. Yes, I will call you later. Goodbye." Tasha finishes her call and hangs up.

"What is it, Scott? It's getting late and I am about to leave."

He turns on her television screen and adjusts his wireless earpiece.

"Okay Chris, route the live feed to her office."

Tasha sits back down in her chair.

"Alright Scott, what are we looking at here?"

"About an hour ago, around eight o'clock our time, one of the tracking teams picked up local, closed circuit footage of one of the Han's. The footage is from a port market place in Southern Hong Kong, in the Guangzhou province."

Tasha's eyes become intrigued and she adjusts herself in her seat.

Scott speaks into his earpiece again, "Bring up the still-frame shots."

Images of a longhaired, Asian female, pop up on the screen beside the live bodycam feed from the operations team on the ground.

"Great, we found the sister. This is great work, Scott."

Scott looks back at her and holds up his hand to her.

"Chris, now zoom in and show the facial recognition comparison of the brother."

A different photo, of an Asian male, aligns on top of the current female image displayed on the screen. A light flashes green, with '98.7% Match' displayed.

Tasha and Scott look at each other in silence for a second.

"Clever boy. So, what's your analysis on this, Scott?"

"The last confirmed sighting before this was near another port in Shanghai, last month. I think that they are trying to find passage on a ship, or maybe gain access to a boat, to sail away from mainland China. Their tactics indicate that they know someone is after them, maybe not us necessarily, but they know someone is watching them. And of course, they know their parents are dead by now. Based off this photo, we know that they are now altering their appearance in public. This is most certainly how they have been able to avoid detection from the general population of Phase Three TSOMBIEs. So, based on that evidence, that is why I also believe that they are...wait...hang on a second."

Scott adjusts his earpiece volume several times.

"Chris. Chris. Yeah, what did you say?"

Scott looks back at Tasha and shakes his head.

"Okay...thanks, Chris...yeah, go ahead and kill the feed then."

The television image turns to static.

"They lost him in the market. Sorry, I thought we had him for sure."

"Scott, do not apologize. It's a sign of weakness. Be confident, and get the job done. We only have a few more left to bring in. And you know how important this is. Get with my assistant on the way out and update the Han 'Wanted Message' package to all TSOMBIE populations throughout Asia, not just China. And have our teams on the ground verify all the rapid scanners along the Asian Pacific seaboards, including all cargo vessels. If we can't get it done with our teams within the next seventy-two hours, I'll request additional agency support through the regional Society headquarters there."

"Understood. I'll get right on it." Scott says, beginning to exit her office.

"Wait. While you are here, do you have any updates on the other remaining bloodlines?"

"No. No updates on the one in Europe or the six remaining here in old America."

"Okay. Well, I have some business at our new Society headquarters over the weekend, so, you can contact me there if you have any further updates."

"Will do." Scott says, as he begins exiting the office again.

"Oh, and Scott, remind your teams that it is kill or capture. We have more than enough non-Society bloodlines for testing and reproductive purposes now."

Scott nods in understanding and shuts the door.

Tasha watches him talk with her assistant outside of her office.

She puts her coat on after sending out one last email, and then leaves the office.

"Have a good night Ms. McNeil," says her assistant.

"Thank you, Rita. You too."

"And, ma'am, your selection for the weekend is already standing by at your home."

"Thank you, Rita. A good night I will have indeed."

FIVE

"Julia," Robert whispers softly into Julia's ear. "Julia. Wake up. I have to tell you something."

Julia moans, "What time is it?"

"Seven. Seven in the morning. Come on, wake up, just for a minute."

Julia moans again and turns over. "Can't it wait? I was having such a good dream. Steak, fresh seafood…"

"Julia," Robert says in a more normal tone, but slightly irritated.

"Okay, okay. Don't cry about it."

Julia rolls back over on her bed and cracks open her eyes, and then tilts the bed lamp away from her face.

"Okay, I'm up. What is it?"

"I did it, Julia. I finally deciphered the last line of code that I have been working on."

Julia's eyes open a little wider.

"Really? I mean, that's great then. So, how many did you open? Are all of them decrypted now?" She asks eagerly, fully awake now.

"Well, no, it is just the one file. But I know that..."

Robert stops talking at Julia rolling her eyes and turning back over, furiously throwing the cover over her head.

"You ruined my steak dinner dream for one file?" She huffs loudly from under the cover.

Robert shakes his head. His feeling of excitement dulls from Julia's somewhat harsh, but honest and appropriate reaction.

"One file. You're right, Julia, that was kind of stupid of me to get so excited about. At this pace, I might get them all open within the next decade. I'm sorry I woke you up for that nonsense sweetie. Go back to sleep."

Julia turns back over and removes the blanket from her face. She realizes what she had said. She realizes her reaction had killed his enthusiasm.

"Hey," She grabs his hand.

He turns slowly back towards her but keeps his head down, upset at the reality of it all.

"I'm sorry I acted like that, Dad. It's great news. Really, it is. Every little bit of progress helps us, right? No matter how small it might seem, right? You told me that, remember? You have been doing great, Dad. Really, don't stop what you are doing."

Robert's mood improves. He raises his head and smiles at her, thinking to himself how lucky he is to have her with him, to have her back again, as his loving and caring daughter.

"Thank you, Julia. That means a lot to me."

"Now then, are you finally going to relax and get some rest now?"

"Yes. Well, almost. I just need to adjust the antennas outside. And we are out of whiskey."

"I'll do that. You need to rest, Dad. I'll get Justin to go with me."

"Are you sure? You don't have to."

"Yeah, it's no problem. I need to get a little bit of exercise in. And, I'm awake now because of 'someone' anyways."

Robert tilts his head to apologize.

"It's okay, I am just messing with you. Now, go to bed old man. I mean it."

"Okay, I will try to get some rest. Don't let me oversleep though."

"You got it."

"Goodnight, sweetheart. Or morning. You know what I mean."

Julia smiles, "Goodnight, Dad."

Julia watches Robert enter his operations room, and continues watching as the ceiling light goes out, with the desk lamp following a few seconds later. Her smile turns into a light yawn as she stands up and stretches.

She walks softly into the kitchen and starts a pot of coffee.

A voice from behind startles her.

"What are you doing up so early? And what were you and Robert talking about?" Justin asks and takes a seat at the table.

He turns on his small electronic game and starts thumbing away.

Julia rolls her eyes and turns back to the coffee and watches it brew. She closes her eyes in pleasure, as the fresh aroma begins to fill the kitchen area.

"He woke me up to tell something, something kind of important. He finished the last line of code he was working on."

Justin pauses the game and looks up at Julia, still facing away from him.

She hears his thumb clicking stop.

"It only worked on one file though."

Justin shakes his head and starts the game back up.

"He woke you up for that? What a prick."

"Come on, Justin. Anyways, I told him that I would get you to help me on a supply run to the cabin."

"Absolutely." Justin immediately turns the game off and walks quickly back to his room. He returns in less than a minute, carrying his rifle and a backpack.

"Alight, I'm ready. Let's go."

Julia turns around to face him while drinking a sip of coffee. She moves her free hand up and down, pointing at her thin layer of clothes, basically her pajamas.

"And, I just started drinking my coffee. Hold your horses there. You act like you are dying to get out of here all the time. The bunker isn't that bad, you know. I mean, it could always be worse, you could be by yourself down here."

Justin takes off the backpack and sits down again, leaning the rifle against the table.

He sits and thinks about what she said and knows that she is right, and he knows that she has more time alone in the bunker than any of them combined. He thinks for another moment about how hard it must have been for her, to be stuck in the bunker for a whole year, by herself.

"Sorry. I'm just ready for a little break from this place."

"No kidding, I could hardly tell." She says jokingly.

They smile at each other and Justin picks the game back up.

"Alright Justin, give me about ten minutes and I'll meet you at the hatch. I need you to wake up Dave before we leave though, we have to adjust the antennas again while we are outside."

"No problem. I'll meet you at the hatch in ten."

*　*　*

"Bravo, this is Alpha, radio check." Julia says into her radio mic, and looks back at Dave though the forest, still barely visible.

"Loud and clear, how me?" Dave responds on the other end.

"Same. Okay Bravo, I'll give you a push when we make it to the site."

"Roger that. I will be standing by. Good luck and be safe out there."

Dave sits down at the opening of the hatch, on the top step, just inside the circular hatch door. He watches as Julia and Justin completely disappear from his eyesight, and further into the woods. He picks up the small, FM radio and puts it in his lap.

The radio is connected to a long cable running down the steps, and then the cable disappears into an exposed earth section of the bunker wall.

Dave turns on the radio and adjusts the volume and scans the frequency band, but there was just a lot of static on every channel, every channel that was now controlled by The Society.

Julia and Justin stay spread out from each other, as they continue moving through the woods, toward the antenna site.

After about ten more minutes of walking, they stop. Justin removes his backpack and props his rifle against an oak tree and looks up at the small, camouflaged antenna.

"Okay Bravo, we made it. We are on site. Let us know when the static is gone from the signal. Over." Julia keys her mic.

"Copy that Alpha. Standing by." Dave says, holding the FM radio closer to his ear.

Justin springs up the tree like a wild cat, chasing its prey. In just a few movements, he reaches the concealed antenna about thirty feet up, and begins making adjustments.

"Okay, that's good Alpha. I've got a clear radio signal now."

"Roger that Bravo."

Julia tosses a small rock at Justin in the tree. "That's good Justin. Secure it."

She keys her radio mic again, "Okay Bravo, lock it up. We will contact you again when we are back at the opening, after we complete our other mission."

"Will do. Be safe out there. And tell Justin not to put too much water back in the vodka bottle." Dave says wittingly, and then begins closing the hatch.

"Thanks, I'll tell him. Alpha out." Julia shakes her head and smiles.

Justin hops down the last six or seven feet from the tree and shakes his shirt off.

"Too easy. I still got some skills. You almost hit me with that rock you know."

Julia smiles and hands Justin his rifle, as he puts on his backpack and smiles back.

They begin walking again.

They are silent for most of the walk, both enjoying the fresh air and morning sunlight.

After several miles of cautious, but peaceful walking, they arrive at the cabin.

They take a knee along the edge of the tree line and observe the cabin for a few moments before walking across the small open area.

They move to the cabin.

Then they start conducting a quick sweep of the interior after they enter, just in case and part of their normal procedure.

All clear.

Julia waves to the small camera hidden in the living room, above the fireplace, signaling everything is okay to Dave, back at the bunker. Then she stands still, almost in a trance, looking at the couch. She thinks about Mr. Roark.

After a few moments of quiet reflection, Justin's rambling through the kitchen cabinets and closets breaks her concentration. She lets out a sigh and regains focus. She moves to the kitchen and storage room area to help Justin pack.

Baby wipes, batteries, and a few cans of coffee began to fill Justin's oversized backpack.

The bunker had more than enough of everything they needed. But Robert wanted to continue depleting the cabin supply every chance they had and move the remaining supplies to the bunker, in the event anyone ever stumbled upon the cabin in the future.

They continue packing and making light conversation, passing each other items to put in the other's backpack as they both start running out of room. The last thing to pack was the monthly ration of alcohol, one bottle.

Justin opens the top cabinet and they both stare in silence at the few dozen bottles of different alcohol, with the majority being whiskey. He pulls down a random bottle of whiskey from the front row and places it in the backpack. Then he stretches his arm deep into the cabinet, pulling it back out with a bottle of vodka, about half empty.

He smiles back at Julia as he opens it up. He closes his eyes and takes a decent size shot.

"Ahh...Whoo! That'll wake you up in the morning."

Justin squirms a little and takes a smaller, normal size shot.

He hands the bottle to Julia.

Julia laughs and takes a small drink from the bottle. She coughs twice and quickly takes a drink of water.

Justin smiles and takes the bottle back.

"One for good luck, and one for the road." He takes two more drinks and offers the bottle back to Julia.

"No thanks, I'm good. Let's start heading back. I want to get back before Brian wakes up. I don't like leaving him with everyone else by himself.

Justin looks at Julia and shrugs his shoulders as if he doesn't care. Then he opens a bottle of water and begins refilling the vodka bottle back to the previous amount that it was at.

"Hey, not too much water," Julia says quickly. "Dave knows about the bottle too."

Justin pauses, somewhat surprised, and then adds another small drop of water and smiles to himself. He puts the vodka back in the cabinet and stares at Julia.

"What?" He asks.

Julia is still thinking about Brian, not Justin's sneaky tactics with the alcohol.

"Look, I know it seems a burden to put up with Brian, Justin. I know. But, regardless of how he is now, he is still..."

"He is still our family. I know. You did the right thing, Julia." Justin pats her on the shoulder. "Come on, let's go."

"Thanks, Justin. Yeah, let's go."

She follows Justin out of the backdoor and then stops, just before closing the door completely.

She stares back at the couch once more. Never forgotten.

* * *

"Good morning handsome."

Dave turns around from the computer monitor and whispers, "Not so loud. Robert is still sleeping."

Amy looks over Dave's shoulder at the dim outline of Robert, lying on the bed in the corner of the operations room. She leans in closer and gently kisses Dave on the cheek.

They smile at each other and then they look quietly at the live CCTV footage on the monitor. They continue watching for a few moments until Justin and Julia disappear into the woods, heading back to the bunker.

Dave stands up slowly and they both exit the room quietly. They walk into the kitchen area.

"What time did they go on the supply run?"

"A couple of hours ago. Is Samantha still sleeping?

"Yep. It's just you, and me."

"What about Brian?"

"Sleeping." Amy smiles and walks slowly toward him, unbuttoning her shirt.

They begin to kiss.

"You guys think Samantha needs a little brother or something?"

Amy shrouds behind Dave and quickly buttons up her shirt. Dave blushes a little and shakes his head.

"Sorry, Robert. We thought you were sleeping."

"Yeah, I got a few hours in. I'm as good as new now. Morning Amy."

"Robert," she replies. She rolls her eyes at Dave and then returns to their bedroom.

"Are they on their way back? I didn't see them on the monitor." Robert asks Dave.

"Yeah, they just started heading back from the cabin."

"And the antenna?"

"Fixed. All the ANN and AGI channels are clear as a bell again."

Robert nods at Dave as he empties the last bit of coffee from the pot and then begins making a bowl of oatmeal.

Dave takes a seat and waits for Robert to finish fixing his food.

"Mm, mm, breakfast of champions right here."

"So, Robert, are we really going to initiate contact with the others today?

"That's the plan." Robert mumbles, with a mouthful of oatmeal.

"Do you think…do you think they are still…well, you know…"

Robert looks up from his bowl of oatmeal and waits for Dave to finish the sentence, already knowing what it is.

"...I mean, what's the plan if...if they don't answer?"

Robert begins eating again.

"Let's just try calling everyone first, okay? And then go from there."

"Yeah.   Sorry.   I'm just ready to do something you know, anything."

Robert looks up from his bowl again.

"Alright, Dave. Go ahead and grab the box of phones and start checking batteries. Then, I guess you can go ahead and start making calls outside the hatch."

Dave begins grinning like a kid on Christmas morning.

"You got it boss."

"Julia and Justin will be back soon anyways, so have them give you a hand out there. I'm going to read through the new file I deciphered and figure out what it means and how it can help us."

Dave smiles and nods.

Robert's smile fades after Dave leaves the room. He begins thinking about what was on the tip of Dave's tongue about the contacts. He knew that everyone in the bunker was thinking the same thing, were the contacts still alive? And he knew that they would all find out the answer, soon.

SIX

Tasha walks down the long hallway of the new headquarters building, toward the oval office.

Two security guards stand outside the office door. The guards lower their heads robotically in respect to Tasha as she approaches, and then open the door for her.

Mr. Hardy motions for her to come in and have a seat near his desk, while he continues talking on the phone.

"Right...No, I don't think that will be too difficult to make happen...Right...Thank you again for your support, and we look forward to seeing you next month for the tour of the new headquarters...Okay...You too."

Mr. Hardy hangs up his office phone and lets out a deep breath of frustration.

"Well, it is going to cost us, but I think we can count Smith as a solid vote."

"Really? I thought that he would stay with Trip James."

"No, no. Miranda Smith. From bloodline seventeen."

"Oh. Well, that's good news sir."

"It is, and that brings our total to six that are committed to give me their vote. But, we still have a long way to go before we can relax here."

"Don't worry sir, we will get there."

Mr. Hardy smiles at Tasha as he takes a seat at his desk.

"So, what updates do you have for me today?"

Tasha leans over and places a binder in front of him, opening it up on top of his desk.

"I have the election communication package for the public that you asked for. It's ready for your final review. It will be ready for immediately release following the old President's future resignation broadcast and address to the Nation. A copy of both versions of the message is in the first folder right there."

"Okay, I will look over it again."

"In the second folder, you will find the current significant events on the non-Society bloodlines. We are closing in on the Han siblings. The targeting and surveillance department was recalled yesterday, and began mass, non-stop monitoring of all the search teams on the ground. I have also coordinated to have another company of military personnel to be repurposed in that general area. And, an additional plane, full of our field agents, also landed on site, just earlier this morning. The brother and sister will be captured, or killed, within the next seventy-two hours, sir. I can guarantee you of that."

Mr. Hardy looks up from the folder and raises his greyish eyebrows at her last remark.

Tasha reaffirms her statement of confidence, "I guarantee it, sir."

Mr. Hardy nods and closes the binder. He picks up his coffee and walks over to the sofa, taking a seat beside Tasha.

"Now, let's talk about the more relevant matter at hand. At what point do we finally pull the pin on the temporary immune Society bloodlines, and begin their Phase One through Phase Three injections to convert them?"

Tasha and Hardy share a moment of devilish and crooked grins, as they both envision a truly exclusive and elite reign, once and for all. And that time was now very close in sight.

SEVEN

"Boys, come say bye to your father."

Mike finishes his breakfast and smiles at his wife, yelling from the foyer. He picks up his briefcase and walks over to her.

"Another great weekend with all of us together, over already." She says, giving Mike a hug and a kiss.

Their sons run down the stairs and hug Mike around his waist. He smiles at them and Melissa and enjoys the moment.

"Bye, Dad," his sons say at the same time.

"Have a good day at work, babe."

"Yuck. She said babe." The oldest, Jack says.

Mike rolls his eyes slightly and Melissa smiles at him as he walks out the door.

*   *   *

There is an unusual roar of commotion as Mike enters the targeting and surveillance department, filled with an unusual, enormous number of analysts.

He walks to his desk through an orchestra of controlled chaos, with Scott Barnes directing a large-scale operation from the center of the room. Mike drops his briefcase at his desk and stops a Phase Three analyst walking by him.

"Hey you, stop. What's going on right now? Why are all shifts of analysts here? What operation is going on right now?"

The analyst stops and answers Mike very calmly, almost robotically. "Sir, we are conducting a non-Society bloodline operation. The Hans, both the brother and sister, have been captured in Asian and are currently being brought in. Is there anything else, sir?"

Mike makes a bee-line though the crowded department floor, straight to Scott at the main control center.

Mike hovers over him, as Scott continues to talk into a headset, systematically and giving several sets of directions and orders. Mike begins to interrupt him but Scott motions for him to wait, holding his hand out.

Mike scoffs with impatience and then he looks up at the big screen and watches the live bodycam feed from one of the agents on the ground. He sees the male Han being loaded onto a medical stretcher, blood covering his torso.

Mike looks away and glares at his old assistant, Chris.

Chris immediately looks away, avoiding any confrontation with Mike.

Mike looks back at Scott, infuriated now, and grabs Scott by the arm.

Scott removes the headset.

"Yeah, what do you need, Mike? I'm pretty busy right now."

"What do I need? For one, why wasn't I notified about this op?"

Scott hesitates to answer him and looks to Chris for some type of support, who quickly looks away again.

"Can we please talk about this later, Mike? I promise I will fill you in, once everything settles down and we are all clear."

Scott puts his headset back on and reaches for the control panel.

Mike grabs his hand, stopping him.

"Why wasn't I notified? Tell me, Scott."

"Look, it wasn't my call, Mike. I'm sorry. Now, can you let me do my job, please?"

Mike lets go of Scott's hand, and he immediately knows that it was Tasha who made the call to keep him out of the operation.

Mike storms out of the department and heads upstairs.

A secretary stands and greets Mike as he approaches Tasha's office. "Good Morning Mr. Hardy. Ms. McNeil is not…"

Mike swings open Tasha's office door to an empty room. He turns back to the secretary he just ignored.

"Where is she?"

"Ms. McNeil is in a meeting, sir."

Mike storms back down the hall.

A security guard addresses him as he approaches the conference room. "Sir, there is a meeting in progress. Only authorized personnel are…"

"Stand down! That's an order from a Society member." Mike pushes the Phase Three guard out of the way and bursts through the doors.

"So, now I don't even get notified of operations? I am not going to just stand by quietly and let you do this to me!"

Tasha spins her chair to the right and stares quietly at Mike, standing in the doorway.

They stare at each other intensely for a few brief seconds. Tasha grinds her teeth and turns back around to the small group in the room, and on the television screens.

Everyone in the meeting looks up briefly, trying not to stare too long at Mike or Tasha during this awkward moment.

"Ladies and gentlemen, I am sorry for the inconvenience. But, we will have to continue this meeting at a later time and date. My sincerest apologies."

Mike stands there in the doorway. Motionless. His heavy breathing now somewhat steady, but his face is still boiling red.

Mike and Tasha stare at each other intensely again, while the members in the room quickly exit the uncomfortable confrontation.

The television screens go blank.

Mike waits for the room to completely empty and then walks over to Tasha. He slams his hands down on the large conference table in front of her, sending her papers flying softly in the air.

"I will not let you push me out of my own department!"

Tasha smirks at Mike's display of authority, but she is not impressed.

"Your department? It is not 'your' department anymore, Mike." Tasha says sarcastically, and then opens her eyes extremely wide. "Wait a second. Wow! This is so strange. This feels like Déjà vu. Hmm, weird. Yes, I feel like I have told you that before, like over three months ago maybe, when Scott was placed in charge of 'your' department."

She looks at Mike sternly, waiting for his response.

Mike snaps back into reality from his brief fit of rage and passion.

She is right, he thinks to himself. It is not my department anymore, and it hasn't been for some time now.

Mike walks over to the large windows and lets out a deep sigh.

He looks over his shoulder after a moment of reflection. "You can't get rid of me completely, Tasha. I am still a Hardy at the end of all this, and that still means something."

Tasha smirks again, tapping her red fingernails gently on the table.

"You're right, Mike. I can't kick you out completely. Not yet anyways. But, you and I both know that the Hardy dynasty is finished after your father steps down. And until that time, your father has appointed me to run AGI. So, remember this, I control what goes on here, me. And it is only a matter of time before your father and the board officially announce me as second in command of The Society, regardless of who wins the upcoming election. An election that should never have to happen in the first place."

Mike turns back around toward the windows and looks down at the floor, without responding.

Tasha gets up and walks to the door.

"And Mike, remember this too, if you don't like how I run things here, the door is always open should you choose to walk out on you own terms. And like you said, you are still a Hardy at the end of this. You don't need to do anything great. You can just live happily ever after by riding on the legacy coattails of other great men within your family. Now, if you will excuse me, I need to get an update on 'my' operation in progress."

Mike looks up and just stares at her, speechless, with no words that could match hers.

Tasha smiles at him with pride from her own remarks for a few seconds, soaking in her arrogance, and then she leaves the room.

He takes a seat after she leaves. Beaten, once again. Humiliated, once again.

He looks to the ceiling and thinks quietly to himself, searching for answers, alone in his thoughts. Maybe she's right? If I am not going to take over, what's the point? Why don't I just give up and quit?

EIGHT

"And nothing, again. Can you pass me another phone, please? I got another battery dying over here." Dave says, dropping a phone on the ground.

Julia reaches in the metal box, full of disposable phones, and hands one to Dave. Then she looks at Justin lying on the ground, looking up at the sky.

She chucks a phone across the bunker hatch and it hits Justin square in the chest.

"Stop," Justin drools out, in a bored and unemotional tone.

"Keep trying, Justin. Come on, it's going to get dark out here soon. We have to keep trying." Julia says, holding a phone to her ear.

"Keep trying? Keep trying? Are you kidding me right now? I have dialed so many numbers today that I actually have blisters starting to form on my fingers now. Look." Justin holds his hand in the air. "I have tried, okay. I tried half of the day yesterday, and I have tried all day today. How much more would you like me to try, Julia? How much more, huh?"

A moment of silence goes by.

Julia throws her phone back in the box, somewhat upset. She is not upset by Justin's rude voice, she is upset about the fact that what he said was true, and that was upsetting in and of itself to think about.

Justin sits up. "Hey, I'm sorry Julia. I didn't mean to take it out on you."

Julia looks at Justin, seeing he is sincere, and nods in acceptance of his apology.

"But Julia, don't you think something is wrong here? I mean, not one, not one single contact has answered."

Julia doesn't respond to him and she looks at Dave.

Justin looks at Dave too. "Dave, come on man, you're thinking the same thing I am, right? I mean, I can't be the only one here."

Dave looks back over at Julia, her head now hanging down. "Drop it, Justin." He looks to Julia. "We'll try again tomorrow, right?"

"No, Dave, it's okay. Justin is just saying what we have all been thinking."

Dave looks at Justin and shakes his head at him for starting this.

"It does not mean that they are dead, necessarily," Julia continues. "But, for not a single person to answer, after all of our attempts…well, that definitely means that something has changed out there. Which in turn means that our plans need to change, for down here."

They all look at each other quietly for a moment, as the sun begins to set over the trees in the forest.

"Whoa. Whoa. Hold on a minute. Hold on." Justin echoes himself as if he just witnessed something majestic. "You're talking about back out there again, aren't you?"

They all look at each other, once again in silence, and in understanding.

Justin gets up and begins packing up and gathering phones, shaking his head and mumbling somewhat nervously to himself. "You might be right, but I don't think Robert will go for it. No way he will go for it. But, I guess we will find out. I mean, we have to ask him. We have to."

Julia and Dave both look at each other after Justin's remarks. Dave tilts his head a little back at her.

They stop talking and continue packing.

Julia and Dave don't say anything else, out there or on the way back inside. They just walk and listen to Justin, as he keeps rambling and mumbling on their way back down into the bunker.

* * *

Amy comes in the kitchen to the commotion of Justin's voice, mixed with opening and closing of cabinets.

Justin sits the bottle of liquor down on the table as she walks in.

"Hey sweetie. How did it go today?" Amy says.

Dave shakes his head to her question.

She kisses him gently on the cheek. Then she looks at the expression on Julia's face. She recognizes it. It is the same look that she had on her face when Julia told them that they had to leave the cabin.

Amy awakens from her thoughts, knowing that there is something else that hasn't been said yet. But she doesn't want to ask them.

Amy clears her throat. "I'll start on dinner for you guys then, you must be starving. And keep your voice down, Justin. Samantha is taking a nap. I think Robert is too."

"Sorry."

"Justin apologizing? Man, what did I miss?"

Robert's shadow emerges from the far end of the kitchen. He puts his hands on the top of Julia's shoulders.

She touches one of his hands softly, and then pulls it back.

Everything goes quiet and Robert notices the bottle on the table.

"Well, I would say this is cause for celebration." He picks up the bottle and puts it back down. "But, judging by the awkward wave of silence and looks on your faces, I take it that there is something else. Am I right?"

Nobody answers.

"We have called everyone, Robert. We have called hundreds of times over the past two days. And nobody has answered. Nobody." Justin says boldly, and then waits for his response.

Robert lets out a slow, deep breath, and leans back against the countertop.

"Okay. This is definitely not going as we originally planned then." He looks around the table, Julia and Dave still have their heads down. "Is that it?"

"Tell him, Julia." Justin says calmly.

Julia stares up at Justin, saying nothing.

"Fine. I will tell him." Justin says, and keeps looking at Julia. "Julia thinks we should go back out there. That we need to find out what is happening…or what has already happened."

There is a moment of silence, and then Amy slams a can down and walks quickly out of the kitchen, wiping her face.

"Amy." Dave reaches out to Amy and she smacks his hand away as she walks past him.

Robert takes a seat. He reaches for the bottle and slowly pours a drink. He smiles at Julia, "I agree with Julia."

Julia smiles back softly as Robert takes a drink.

"You agree?" Justin asks.

"Yes, I agree. Something out there is interfering with our plans. And we need to find out what that something is. And...we need to know if they are still alive, or if they are...dead. Plain and simple. And I would be lying if I said that I have not already thought about it, especially after nobody answered their phones yesterday."

Robert takes another drink. "We have to find out."

Julia looks at Justin and can tell he has mixed emotions about the decision. She feels the same way but knows that it has to be done.

Dave looks across the table at Robert, "I want to go, Robert."

"Me too, Dad." Julia says.

"Hold on now, let's just take a minute and think about this, alright? I mean, we are really going to have to work out the details on this one. One mistake, one slip-up, and that's it. It is going to be a lot different out there this time. Phase Three is in full effect now and has been for several months. Which means it will be harder for us to move undetected. But, the time to do it is now. The longer that we wait, the greater the chance that we will get caught. And if the others are in danger, and if they need our help, then the longer we wait...well, the less chance they have to survive. And ultimately, the bottom line is that we need to know if they are in fact, alive or dead. I don't want to us to keep wondering about that for years and years to come down here, and I know none of you do either. So, there are really only two options left for us at this point. We can sit here and do nothing, living out the rest of our days safely in this bunker. And more than likely never finding out what happened to them. Or, we can take a chance, and go back out there to find out what is going on. And risking our own lives in the process."

They all look at each other, all understanding what is at stake, and what they must do. And they all know that everyone is in agreeance. They must go out.

"Let's all eat dinner for now, and then get a good night of sleep. Then, we can start planning first thing in the morning, fresh." Robert finishes in a somewhat, uplifting tone, trying to lighten the dump truck of burden that was now parked on top of everyone's shoulders.

NINE

A doorbell rings.

Nichole rolls over and pulls the cover over her head. Her long, dark blonde hair covers her eyes and face under the cover.

Her doorbell rings again, followed by a series of quick knocks. She rolls her eyes and gets out of bed. She takes a quick look in the mirror and pulls her hair back. She smiles back at herself modestly, at her preserved beauty in her late thirties.

The doorbell rings again and the knocking continues, and she makes her way to the front door.

She recognizes the voice outside her door before she opens it.

"Nikki. Nikki. Open the door."

She cracks open the door, squinting at the morning sunlight, now in her face.

"Come on, Brent. It's seven o'clock in the morning for crying out loud. What do you want?"

The middle-aged man pushes the door open and walks straight past her and into her house.

Nichole huffs as the short, half-bald man bypasses her at the door.

"Sure, come in."

She closes the door and follows behind him. She sits at the kitchen table and watches him, as he rumbles through her cabinets and starts making coffee.

"You're out of sugar again." Brent says, as he continues to open and close cabinet doors, waiting for the coffee to finish brewing.

"Brent. Brent!"

He closes a cabinet and looks back at her, adjusting his eyeglasses and squinting a little.

"What are you doing here this early, Brent? Why did you wake me up?"

"Sorry." He says, beginning to walk towards her.

The coffee spurts, and he turns back around.

"Hang on, just a second. I can't wait to tell you this." He pours what coffee has brewed into two cups and takes a seat in front of her, handing her a cup.

Nichole watches him take a drink, and he immediately makes a bitter facial expression. His jumpy and erratic movements begin to irritate her even more.

"Well? What is it?"

"Oh, right. Sorry, I haven't slept much. So, late last night, I hear trucks driving up and down the street. I didn't think anything of it at first, but they just kept coming and going. So, I go outside to see what was going on, and I see what they were doing. They were setting up another house with furnishings and electricity, in the middle of the night. And of course, I thought it was weird, so I called Richard. And he confirmed it, they were setting up the house another immune."

"After this long? Wow, still alive?" Nichole takes a sip of coffee and begins thinking.

"I know. It's amazing, right? I mean, she was able to hide for such a long time without getting caught or killed. I can't wait to meet her and find out what she is like. To find out what she knows and how she did it."

"She? So, Richard already received his brief, from them?" Nichole's eyes shift to behind Brent, at the camera in her kitchen, aimed at her table.

"Yep. Well, most of it anyways. Her name is Lilly...Lilly Han, I think? Chinese. And it's just her. She is the last of her bloodline. Anyways, she is supposed be here within the hour and Richard wants us all at the welcome center. So, come on, you have to get dressed."

"Yeah. Yeah. Give me a few minutes. Hang on, I need to call mom first."

"I'll go wake Aunt Evelyn up. I need to get some sugar for this coffee anyways. I will be waiting for you outside, and we can just all ride together."

Nichole, now feeling somewhat excited by the news and Brent's enthusiasm, walks quickly to her bedroom and begins changing clothes.

* * *

"Alright everyone, please take a seat." A man in his mid-forties says loudly, standing at the front of a small theatre-like room, filled with seats and a large projection screen in the front. The man, somewhat muscular and well built, runs his hand through his straight, light brown hair and waits for the room to settle down.

The loud chatter around the room dwindles down, and the small groups of people begin to separate and take their seats.

"Thank you. Now, I know everyone is excited to meet our new arrival, but I have some general background information to brief everyone on first." The man looks at the small index card and begins reading. "Name, Lilly Han. Age, twenty-nine. Nationality, Chinese. Multilingual. She studied fashion design in London before working for her father's real estate business. And well, like a few of in here, she is unfortunately the last of her bloodline."

He pauses for a moment.

"I am really not at liberty to talk anymore about her family. She can talk about that with you, when, and if she chooses. Now, I have already spoken to her this morning, and she is still pretty shaken up. So, we are going to cut the welcome brief short today and do the full brief and tour at a future date and time. Standard protocol for this morning. Everyone will briefly introduce themselves, and then I will just ask for Nikki to standby at the end, to help go over some other details with her. Alright, I'm going back to get her."

Richard exits the room. The group looks around at each other in anticipation, hope. Hope, that she might have some answers to their many questions.

Richard slowly opens an office door, "Lilly, it's me again. We're ready for you."

She looks at him and shakes her head no. Her eyes red, swollen and watery.

He takes a knee beside her chair.

"Look, I know what you are going through right now, being the last member of your family. So am I. I know it is hard. But, this is part of the process." He squeezes her hand gently and aims his eyes to the camera above them.

She moves her teary eyes toward the camera, and she understands what he said.

Richard escorts her slowly into the large room.

She pauses at the sight of all the faces in the crowd, all looking at her. She looks back at Richard and shakes her head again.

Richard holds her arm gently, and motions for someone in the front row of seats to come forward.

An older lady, somewhere in her late sixties to early seventies, walks up first to introduce herself.

"Hello dear, I'm Evelyn Phillips." The lady hugs Lilly sincerely for a few seconds.

"This is my daughter, and my nephew. Nichole and Brent."

"Hi, you can just call me Nikki."

"Hey. I'm Brent. It is really nice to meet you. I've got so many questions that I…"

Nichole smiles and jerks on Brent's shirt to stop talking and keep moving.

Richard motions for Nichole not to leave. She positions herself by the door.

The rest of the group begins coming up to introduce themselves and a line starts forming.

Lilly's eyes dry about halfway through the group.

Nichole watches on and tries to imagine what it must have been like to be out there that long, surviving on the run.

"Okay. Now, that wasn't so bad was it?" Richard says to Lilly after the last introduction is made.

He smiles at her and then motions for Nichole to come back up.

"Nikki here, will be your sponsor. She will help with you getting settled in, and with whatever else you might need. And of course, you can always contact me for anything as well."

He turns to Nichole.

"Go over the basics with her, at her pace. And contact me when you get home, or if you have any issues."

Nichole nods and waits for Richard to leave the room.

She tries to think of what to say. She turns back to Lilly and smiles, "Well, looks like it's just us here now."

She offers Lilly a seat.

"I wish he would have given me a heads up, I could have been better prepared. I've never really sponsored anyone before, he's always done that."

She smiles at Lilly and waits for a response, but Lilly just sits there silent.

"Well, there's a welcome video that we all have to watch when we get here, so I guess we can do that first. And then we can just go from there."

She waits for a response again, and again there is nothing from Lilly.

Nichole walks over to the computer near the door.

After a few moments of typing, a video starts playing on the projector screen.

Nichole dims the lights by the door.

"Congratulations on being selected into The Society Integration Program for non-Society members. And welcome to your new home and community within The Society. You are an important asset for the progress and future of The Society, and for the new America. Imagine the greatness people can achieve if someone forces their hand. This was the principle that our founding fathers of The Society started with, and it still remains true today. While here, you are expected to adhere to the community guidelines as outlined in your welcome packet. Your community leader will further assist you in your transition. Again, welcome to your new home within The Society."

The projector screen goes blank and Nichole turns the lights back on.

"Okay. Well, I guess I can show you around now. If you want? Or we can…" She stops talking at the sight of Lilly sleeping, still sitting completely upright in the chair.

She leans in closer to her. "Umm…Lilly?" She places a hand on her shoulder and Lilly awakens, startled.

"Sorry. I'm sorry. Umm, okay, well I think it might be best if you just get some rest now. You look like you could really use it. And don't worry, we can do all this in-processing stuff later, when you are feeling up to it. Come on, I'll take you to your new living quarters."

* * *

Nichole drives Lilly across the repurposed military base to her new home.

Other than the perimeter walls, and noticeable presence of security guards, the base looked like any other small town in America.

After a short drive, with no conversation, Nichole parks in a driveway near the end of a peaceful street of houses. All similar in size. One story, small front and back lawns, with some variation in light, pastel colors on the wood and vinyl siding.

They exit the car and Nichole stops, and points back up the street.

"My house is about halfway up the street there, the white one with the brown SUV in the driveway beside it. Everyone, like us, live along this street. Richard lives in the first house at the beginning of the street. He was the first one here. He has been here the longest. The others, mainly Phase Three employees and security guards, live on the other side of the base. There are only a few, low-level Society members that live on the base. So, for us, it's pretty relaxing on our street here. As much as it can be I guess."

Lilly looks at the houses and her new neighbors, several of them outside.

Nichole waves at a few people standing outside, two houses over.

Lilly stares at a small boy on a bicycle, sitting at the end of her driveway now, looking back at her. A large Golden Retriever by his side. The moment is interrupted by the sound of Nichole opening the door behind her.

Lilly follows her into the house and closes the door. She looks around the somewhat large living room and adjacent kitchen, fully furnished with all of the necessary amenities.

Nichole watches her, and she sees that Lilly begins noticing all the cameras, in almost every corner of the house.

"Don't worry, you will get used to them, eventually. The bathrooms are really about the only place to enjoy a moment of privacy. At least we are left with some type of dignity."

Nichole waits for a response from Lilly, a smile or something, but there is nothing. Nichole moves around the kitchen and opens the refrigerator, conducting a quick inspection of the contents. Then, she closes the refrigerator and walks over to Lilly, still standing in the same spot.

"Everything is fully stocked in the refrigerator for you. Meat, vegetables, soda, snacks. And the cabinets are stocked with all of the cookware you need, as well as some other things like nonperishables."

She pauses and still there is no response from Lilly.

"There are clothes in your bedroom closets and dressers. It's just down the hallway there, all of our houses are designed pretty much the same." Nichole points. "And over here, are all of your communication devices. Home phone, cell phone, a couple of tablets, and a computer. There is a list somewhere around here though…"

Nichole stops talking and begins searching through a desk drawer for a moment.

"Here it is. All of our numbers are on here."

Lilly walks over and touches the computer keyboard softly, and then she looks back at Nichole with confusion.

"All of the communication devices are on a closed network here. So, it's not what you think. We can only communicate with each other, and of course, them."

Lilly's look of confusion disappears, and she clearly understands.

"Everything you do is being watched. Everything you say is being heard." Nichole glances at the cameras in the corner again. "But like I said before, you will eventually get used to it."

They look at other in silence for a moment.

"I know Richard already told you, but there is no escaping this place. Even if you did get out, I mean you know better than any of us what it's like out there, it is not the same. All of the normal people that are left are right here, together, and we are safe here. This is a good life here, Lilly. This really is best life for us now."

Nichole shifts her eyes to the cameras around them, and slowly nods her head. Lilly blinks her eyes slowly and nods back in understanding, of Nichole's somewhat coded message.

"Alright, I am going to leave so that you can get some much-needed rest."

Nichole smiles and starts walking to the door. "Oh, and don't be surprised if people from the neighborhood come over to talk your head off. You are kind of a miracle. I mean, to survive that long, alone. Well, it's pretty incredible. Alright, I've talked enough. Bye."

Lilly looks out of the window and watches Nichole drive back up the street. She sees several people outside looking at her house and she closes the curtains.

She walks slowly through the house, opening all of the doors and turning the lights on and off. She opens the last bedroom door. Bed. Chester drawers. Small desk. There is paper and several Society pamphlets and books on top of the desk.

She picks up the writing pad and begins drawing something. Within five minutes she had drawn a rough sketch of her brother's face.

She lies down on the bed, placing the sketch on the pillow beside her.

Physically and mentally exhausted from the past twenty-four hours of her drastically changed life, Lilly closes her eyes and falls fast asleep.

TEN

Julia, Justin, and Dave, all sit patiently, waiting for Robert to finish plotting thumbtacks and notes on the map against a wall in his operations room.

Robert takes a step back from the wall and looks over the map for a moment, studying the vast array of information. He turns and faces the group. Anticipation covering their faces, with a slight hint of worry.

"So, we already know that the longer we stay out there, the chances of us getting caught increases. The routes I have plotted for us this time are different from the previous ones, mainly because the old routes were too long to go from point to point, like Julia did before. So, we are going to split up into teams this time. We can cover more ground that way, and we will be faster. And that reduces the risk of all of us getting caught at one time. But splitting up is also not without risk. We all won't be there to help one another, should we get into trouble."

Robert pauses for a moment and they all look at each other, all on the edge of the couch now.

"Julia, Justin. You two are together. Midwest and the West Coast."

Julia and Justin look at each other.

Dave looks at Robert and smiles, happy that he will be pairing up with Robert.

"Just like old times, huh Robert?" Dave says, smiling.

Robert looks away and down at the floor and Dave's smile begins to fade away.

"I will be taking the East." Robert says, looking up at Dave. "Alone."

Dave closes his eyes and shakes his head, and then Robert walks over and places a hand on his shoulder.

"Dave, listen…if something happens to me, or Justin and Julia out there, 'we' still have something of value to offer them." Robert points to Julia, Justin, and himself. "Our blood is immune, yours is not. Maybe they kill us, maybe they don't. But for you, it would be worse than death. You know that. First, they would inject you with all phases of shots at once, which would certainly kill you within a few days, if not sooner. But before you died, they would make you tell them everything you knew. Where this bunker was at. Where your wife and kid were at. And then…well, you can only imagine how they would kill you if the injections didn't kill you first. You and your family are the only ones that are not immune that know about this bunker. Tommy knew, but…well, you have to understand my point here Dave. Don't you?"

Dave doesn't like it, but he knows that Robert is right. He nods quietly and then looks at him. "What about you though, Robert? I mean, by yourself?"

"Yeah Dad. Come on, let's just all go together. Yes, it will take longer, but we will be safer together."

"I agree with Julia." Justin says quickly.

"Guys, guys. This is not up for debate. Okay?"

Julia and Justin both slump back into the couch.

"And I know that I might be a little older now, but I am in just as good of shape as Justin. So, you don't have to worry about me out there. I will be fine."

Justin laughs softly at Robert's fitness comment.

Everyone stares at him with raised eyebrows.

Justin clears his throat and tries to play off the laugh like his throat is dry, reaching for a drink of water.

They all grin a little, and the mood in the room changes to a more positive one, from worrisome to lighthearted and comfortable.

Julia notices Brian out of the corner of her eye through the operations doorway, sitting down in the kitchen by himself.

"I'll be back in a minute." Julia walks out of the room quickly and into the kitchen.

"Hey Brian. You hungry?"

Brian shakes his head yes, and then continues playing a small handheld game, just like the one that Justin plays all the time.

Julia heats up some water and makes him a bowl of oatmeal. She puts a couple of leftover canned peaches on top of the oatmeal. She sits the bowl in front of him and rubs her hand softly through his hair.

He looks up at her with a blank expression, and then he continues playing the game.

Julia pulls her hand back and lets out a sigh. She gently pats him on the shoulder and walks back to the operations room.

Julia notices a set of identification cards on the table as she takes a seat. She looks at Justin holding up a set of cards as well. She picks up her cards and scans through them all.

One set was an AGI analyst. One set was a reporter for ANN. And one set was just normal licenses, one for each of the states they would be traveling to with contacts in them.

They were all similar to the previous fake identifications like she had used before, when she was traveling as Dr. Gordon. But there was one thing about these cards that was noticeably, and drastically different.

"Steve Smith? Really?"

Justin begins laughing but stops himself as soon as Julia snaps a fist of air at him.

"Well, I have some more names to choose from Julia. But you are going to need to impersonate a man this time. That is the best way to conceal your identity from facial recognition."

"So, Justin is going as a woman then? Right?"

"No way." Justin says, shaking his head.

"Justin could never pull that off." Dave laughs.

"So, what are you trying to say about me then?" Julia stares at everyone

"Look, it's not like that okay. You're a beautiful woman, and everyone here knows that. All I am saying, is that with a short haircut, fake facial hair, and the right clothes, it is much easier for you to blend in as a male. We can add male features a lot easier than trying to cover them up, and that's just the simple truth. Justin will wear a fake nose and chin, and we will change his hair color and facial hair as well. So, can we move on with our planning now?"

Julia accepts the answer and nods.

Justin runs his fingers over his nose and chin.

They sit quietly and listen as Robert starts briefing the details of their operation, and then they begin planning every step of their new mission. The playfulness subsides, and everyone gets serious, knowing the consequences that would come from any of their shortcomings.

* * *

The detailed planning and training continues for the next two days in the bunker. They perfect their cosmetic disguises. They study their fake bios and background information. They train and retrain on how to act like they are Phase Three again, whenever they see cameras, or come in contact with the TSOMBIE population, or even worse, Society members.

Robert struggles with the thought of having to put his decryption work on the files on hold, until he makes it back to the bunker at least. He does not want to take the chance of Dave trying to continue the decryption work and possibly ruining the progress somehow.

Julia spends her little free time over the next couple of days with Brian. She tries to explain to him that she will be gone for a while, and even though he comprehends what she says, he shows no emotional concern for her leaving, or for the possible danger she faces.

Justin's initial hesitation and nervousness about going on the mission fades away. He regains his confidence after he starts training again, and all of the previous training with Robert and skills he was taught, all come back to him.

Dave helps them with the training, as needed. He tries not to over-involve himself too much. He hates the fact that he is not going with them. But Amy could not be happier with Robert's decision, and Dave takes pleasure in his wife's renewed sense of happiness.

The night before they leave the bunker, they all enjoy a peaceful dinner together. Small talk and light laughter fills the bunker air and into the night, before they all lie down to sleep, one last night at home, together.

* * *

Julia wakes up early in the morning, refreshed, and wide awake with calm anticipation of the day that lies ahead. She gets dressed and quietly finishes packing. She kisses Brian on his forehead, as he continues sleeping.

She walks into the kitchen and Justin, Dave, and Robert, are all drinking coffee and checking over their gear.

Justin and Robert look up at Julia and smile, and then continue preparing themselves, checking their bags and weapons.

They all eat breakfast in silence. None of them really have much of an appetite but they all finish their meals.

Dave walks with them to the sliding bunker wall, down the corridor past the operations room and the one that opened to the long tunnel toward the cabin.

They decide to take the tunnel exit instead of the hatch because it put them in closer proximity to their vehicles that were hidden near the cabin.

"Alright. Well, good luck out there guys. I will be here, waiting…and ready, if you need me for anything."

"Thanks, Dave. We aren't going to call the alert phones unless it is an emergency. To give you a head start, like we talked about."

"Got it. Me and Amy will take shifts monitoring the alarms and phones." Dave shakes Robert's hand.

Robert opens the wall and begins walking into the tunnel first.

Justin shakes Dave's hand and pats him on the shoulder, and then follows behind Robert, turning his headlamp on.

Julia looks at Dave and smiles. She hugs him and gives him a small kiss on the cheek.

"We'll be fine. Take care of Brian for me."

Dave nods and lets out a small sigh while watching them leave.

Julia joins the other two, now slightly ahead of her, as her light shines on their backs.

Dave lowers his head and closes the wall back, slowly, watching the sets of bouncing headlamp beams fade away into the dark tunnel.

The walk out of the tunnel was much like their breakfast, quiet. They reach the exit after over an hour of walking at a quick and steady pace.

They step out of the cave at the end of the tunnel and look at each other, now surrounded by the calm morning sunlight shining down on their faces, sparkling through the treetops.

They all take a drink of water and enjoy the peaceful scenery for a moment. They finish their small break and continue moving, through the quiet woods and toward the cabin.

The walk to the cabin is at a slower pace than through the tunnel, almost as if they were savoring the last little bit of time together.

They make it to the break in the woods near the cabin.

"Okay, we go our separate ways from here. No need to get emotional or anything, because I will see you both back here in a week." Robert says, looking them in the eyes.

Julia and Justin both look at Robert with a calm sense of trust and confidence. Julia gives him a hug with both arms and he kisses her forehead gently. Justin half hugs him with one arm, the other draped by his side, holding his rifle.

Robert motions for them to start walking. He watches them walk further into the forest, further south of the cabin, and then he heads north, alone.

Justin turns around a few times and waves to Robert before they get completely out of sight.

Julia never looks back, she manages to control her emotions and does not want to take the chance of losing them. She diverts all her focus on the mission instead, knowing from experience that her focus will make all the difference, in living or dying.

ELEVEN

Mike opens his eyes to the sun shining into the bedroom, slightly above his pillow and onto the headboard. He closes his eyes and stretches his arms out as he rolls over, placing one arm on the other half of the bed. He feels the empty pillow beside him and opens his eyes again. He looks at his watch. Eleven in the morning. He takes his wife's pillow and places it on top of his and leans back against the headboard.

"Television. Channel one."

The large wall at the opposite end of the bed comes to life out of the white paint. Images of rapid scanners were being shown in front of an AGI facility on the screen. A reporter from ANN was interviewing Tasha McNeil.

"...And thank you, Ms. McNeil, for that information. And AGI is expected to have these redesigned rapid scanners in all residential homes by the end of this year? Is that correct?"

"Yes, no later than the end of this year. But, with the recent increase in our factory workforce and general labor population, I believe we will beat that projection by months."

"Great. Okay folks, that was an exclusive update from AGI's CEO, Ms. Tasha McNeil. Thank you for watching everyone. Remember to like this story on your social media and tell your friends and family of this update. Back to you at the studios, Ken. Up next we…"

"Comedy movie." Mike says, fed up with watching Tasha flaunt around on television.

A movie title image flashes on the screen and starts playing.

Mike slides down into the bed from the headboard and lets out a deep sigh.

He hears heels of shoes striking the marble floors, echoing from within the house, in between seconds of silence from the movie. His wife.

"Off." He says in a soft voice. The movie keeps playing. "Off." He tries a little louder, still nothing. "Off." The screen fades back to white and blends in with the paint on the wall. He throws his head back into the pillow and closes his eyes.

The bedroom door opens softly.

"Mike? Are you awake?"

His wife walks slowly over to the side of his bed and looks at him, back at the wall, and then she looks at her watch. She shakes her head and begins to walk back out.

Mike grabs her tightly and pulls her into the bed with a quick swoop.

She gasps, "Mike! I knew it. I knew I heard the TV."

Then she bursts into laughs as Mike begins tickling her, briefly. He stops and then they look at each other, smiling.

Her smile fades away soon after, and she squirms away from Mike and sits up.

"Hey, Melissa. What's wrong?"

"Nothing. Everything has been so, perfect, lately. But…"

"But what? Melissa, but what?"

She turns around to him, kicks off her heels and pulls her feet into her lap on the bed.

She holds his hands and Mike sits quietly, waiting for her to speak.

"Look, the past week has been great with you at home and not going to work. But you can't just sit around the house every day and spend 'all' of your time with us. You still need to do a little bit of work, a hobby, or something."

"But I love being here with you guys all day, every day. And I do not have to work. I'm a Hardy. We have enough money to last us and the kids forever, we always will."

"I know that Mike, but I'm not talking about money or us. I am talking about you here. Your potential. Your skills. Your name. I hate to see you throw everything away that you have worked so hard for over the years. Especially now, when you are so close."

Mike leans back against the pillows.

"I was close. But Tasha has worked extra hard to ruin everything that I have ever done for AGI, for The Society."

"And that's just it Mike. I don't want to see her lead The Society in the future any more than you do. And I don't want to see her get the best of you. You are better than her, Mike. You always have been. You need to make everyone else see that."

Mike stares at the bed, doubting himself.

She stops looking at him and hangs her head down at the bed as well.

"If you can't do it for yourself, Mike, then do it for me." Her voice cracks a little and she takes a moment before continuing.

"I know about you and Tasha, Mike." She looks up at him and smiles, fighting back her emotions.

Mike looks at her, his face sulks with heartache.

"How did you...when? How long have you..."

"I have always known, Mike. I found a message from her on your phone, your personal phone, on that night it happened."

"I swear, Melissa, it was just that one time. I never..."

"I know, Mike, I know."

"You do? But, how?" He does not understand why she believes anything he tells her at this point.

"Come on, Mike. You don't think that after all these years of you running the surveillance department, that I never learned anything? Or that I never met anyone you worked with, that could show me how to monitor and track someone?"

She walks to the walk-in closet and comes back a moment later, tossing a phone on the bed. He picks it up and looks at it. He looks at his phone on the nightstand beside him. It is a clone of his cellphone.

"I love you, Mike, for better or worse. Always."

She kisses him gently and leaves the bedroom.

Mike sits on the bed, alone. Alone in thought, digesting everything his wife said to him.

Mike's wife motivates him, and he begins planning on how he could earn his position back in the company, to beat Tasha and regain notoriety from his father, from The Society.

After hours of spit-balling ideas to himself and to his wife, the idea finally comes to him, clear as day. The same thing that cost him everything would be the very same thing that brought it all back. Rawlings.

TWELVE

Nichole sips on an afternoon cup of coffee as she sits on her front porch. She watches the normal buzz of daily activity and traffic on Bataan Street.

Most of the people along Bataan Street were eventually connected back to the five, non-Society bloodlines, from the doctors and scientists that were involved in the World War One TSOMBIE project. Therefore, most of them knew each other, as they were relatives within their own bloodlines. There was still a small number of relatives that were distant and unknown to each other, from divorces and remarried families, adoptions. And, there were a few other exceptions. Dr. Nichols' son, Kenton, was one of those exceptions. Dr. Nichols was a Society member, but he took his own life to avoid being apprehended for helping Rawlings. And his involvement with Robert Rawlings ultimately resulted in his son being captured and held in the community camp of non-Society bloodlines. Lilly Han was another one of these exceptions. Lilly and Kenton were similar in the fact that they were the only ones left in their immune, non-Society bloodlines.

Nichole sees Brent making his way to her house from down the street, as she continues drinking her coffee in her temporary moment of peace.

"Hey." Brent says, bypassing Nichole and going straight into her house. He comes out a few minutes later, with a cup of coffee and a sandwich. He takes a seat in the chair beside her and begins eating after almost spitting a drink of coffee out.

"You are killing me with this coffee, Nikki. I don't see how you drink it all the time with no sugar. I'll just bring you some later today."

"Brent, you know this is my house, right?"

He smiles and then takes another small sip of coffee, looking down the street.

They both sit on the porch and look at Lilly down the street, sitting outside on her steps with a notebook in her lap.

"What do you think she is writing all the time? She's always carrying a notebook around with her. Did she talk to you about anything yet?"

"No, not really. I've tried. I have been stopping by every day, but she hasn't opened up about anything personal yet. I haven't been able to get more than a few words out of her. Whatever happened to her out there must have been pretty rough."

Nichole pauses and takes a drink of coffee.

"She's not writing though, she's drawing. I caught a glimpse of her notebook yesterday when I checked on her."

"Drawing? Drawing what?" Brent asks with curiosity.

Nichole shrugs her shoulders and takes another drink of coffee.

They sit and continue to watch Lilly. They also watch Kenton, riding his bike back and forth past Lilly's driveway.

Lilly looks up at the sound of Kenton's bike hitting the ground. She stops drawing as he walks up to her.

"Hi, I'm Kenton. Do you remember me? Your name is Lilly, right?"

She shakes her head yes and then begins drawing again.

"Can I sit down and watch you draw?"

Somewhat uncomfortable by the thought, she offers him a place to sit beside her.

He smiles and takes a seat. He watches her continue drawing for a few moments before he says anything.

"I'm alone too."

Lilly stops drawing and looks at the young boy.

"Those people there," he says and points to people outside his house. "I live with them, but they are not my real family. The bad people that brought me here said that I had to live with other people here, because I was just a kid. And…nobody else in my family was alive to take care of me. They're nice to me, but I still feel lonely sometimes."

Lilly sits in silence for a moment, imagining if he saw his family killed in front of him too.

"So, I was just thinking that…that maybe I could be your friend? So that you won't be alone."

Lilly smiles. "Yeah. I would like that."

"Cool." Kenton smiles.

"So, Kenton, since we are friends now, can you keep a secret?"

"Yeah." He whispers and leans in closer.

"My name is really pronounced Li-Li, not Lilly." She whispers and smiles. "But just call me Lilly like everyone else, so it's not confusing when you are around other people. It's our little secret now, so don't tell anyone."

Kenton nods and smiles back. He looks at her drawing again.

"You can draw really good. Who is that in your drawing?"

She lets out a small sigh, "My brother."

"Is he?"

She looks at Kenton in silence, but he understands what her eyes were saying, no words are needed.

"Can I look at more of your drawings?"

She carefully hands him the notebook, random papers protruding from the sides.

He accepts the notebook with care, and slowly flips the pages.

Drawings of her brother and parents, her home, and memories of joyful events, all flooding the white sheets of paper with tuneful shading of pencil lead and black ink, no color. But even without color, the drawings were overflowing with life and emotion.

Kenton studies each drawing carefully, controlling his excitement. And Li-Li's watery eyes begin to dry from looking at his colorful face.

"Can you teach me how to draw? I want to draw pictures of my family too. I miss them a lot, especially my dad."

Li-Li smiles and shakes her head yes. "Okay. Hang on and wait right here."

She goes inside her house and comes out a minute later, with a blank notebook and a few pencils.

She helps Kenton begin drawing, and for the first time since her brother died, Li-Li feels something other than sadness.

THIRTEEN

"General James, I have the updated vote pledges, sir." A young officer says.

"Thanks, Paul. Come in and have a seat." The General replies.

General Tristan 'Trip' James earned recognition within The Society for the detailed analysis and research conducted on Dr. Singer, after they had discovered his true identity to be that of Robert Rawlings. General James was able to assist in the discovery through Rawlings' prior military service. General James provided insight to The Society Inner Circle on what type of Soldier that Rawlings was. James also led the interrogations on former Soldiers and supervisors of Rawlings. The Rawlings analysis, along with his decorated service in the military, gave General James the opportunity to move up within The Society. His career in the military had other effects on him as well, effects on him physically. He hid the appearance of his prosthetic leg very well. He walked well, with no limp or unnatural movements. But the shrapnel scars on his neck and bottom right jaw were not so subtle. The scars, coupled with his short hair and deep-staring eyes, were a dead giveaway that he was a battle-hardened Soldier. The James family also had a respectable reputation within the old America, both in the private contracting and government sectors. However, the family only ranked in the bottom third of all Inner Circle bloodlines. This reason alone was the number one disadvantage the General faced as a candidate to lead The Society.

His aide takes a seat and hands him a paper copy of the briefing.

"Sir, we have three votes that are locked in and committed as of now. We have another three that are on the borderline. Mr. Hardy has five pledges that we know of, possibly six, but we have not been able to confirm Smith as a pledge. And Mr. Rockmann is leading by at least one vote, with seven confirmed pledges. So, that leaves a total of seven, possibly eight, Inner Circle votes that are not committed yet."

The General begins preparing a cigar. "Which Smith?"

"Bloodline seventeen, sir."

"So, Roger is still leaning towards me then. Right?"

"No sir, not anymore. I'm afraid that he committed to Rockmann earlier this week. I'm sorry, sir."

"No, don't be. I knew it would happen eventually, especially with the amount of debt Roger was in. Rockmann will take advantage of anyone with financial issues during the elections, so let's find out that information on the other voters as well. That way we can count them out early and focus our efforts somewhere else. And, let's confirm Madeline Smith. And if she has not committed to Hardy yet, then I want to put her at the top of our priority list."

"Yes, sir."

"Because even if we can't get her on our side, it still will not be a total loss, as long as she sticks with Hardy."

"Understood, sir. The next thing to go over with you are the updates to the repurposing of military forces and streamline alignment of the remaining branches. We are finally complete with this initiative, as directed by the board. And the last update, sir…is the update on the reduction in military manpower. Our overall strength has been reduced by over sixty percent now. Another fifteen percent of our force will be lost over the next thirty days, sir."

He pauses for a moment. He waits for a response from General James. Nothing.

"I'm sorry sir, I truly am."

"Paul, let me tell you something. I can live with having my power slowly stripped away from me. I can live with being forced into retiring and remaining at the bottom half of the Inner Circle. But, what I can't live with, and what I will not live with, is living under the continued reign of Hardy. It is time for change, for The Society, and for all of us. I don't care about winning as much as I do about someone different taking over."

"What are you suggesting sir? Some type of alliance, perhaps? With Rockmann?"

The General looks at him and nods, while blowing out a large cloud of smoke from his cigar.

"Yes, perhaps. But it's nothing we need to start on right away, there are still some potential pledges out there. But when the time does come, we need to be sure I am positioned with the 'right' votes. Having most of the swing votes will make me, shall we say, invaluable to Rockmann. Therefore, leaving me with the upper hand and all of the bargaining power."

The young officer smiles in understanding and watches General James walk to the window.

"You know what they say, Paul. If you can't beat them then you should…"

"…Join them, sir."

General James looks back from the window and smiles, "Extort them."

FOURTEEN

Justin and Julia approach their first stop, the Missouri brother's home.

They had made the first leg of their trip without any direct contact, avoiding highways and any unnecessary pit stops. They still witnessed people everywhere along their route. TSOMBIEs. Ordinary, functional, completely zombified citizens. Driving cars. Pumping gas. Eating in restaurants. Working construction. Talking on their phones. Nothing appeared drastically different, but it was. And they could feel it.

The drive to Missouri seemed longer to Julia this time. The distance had increased due to more detours this time, in order to decrease their frequency of passing through highway cameras. But it wasn't just the obvious mileage increase that made the trip seem longer to her. There was an eerie silence along the drive, inside the car. It was coupled with the seemingly normal, but permanently different, outside world. It made her feel as if she were alone, in a vacuum of space. She also felt as if she were floating, unnoticed during a live movie, just moving through, from scene to scene. And nobody in the outside world, or in this surreal movie she was floating through, even recognized she was there. There was an indescribable difference in the outside world, from the time between when Phase Two and Phase Three was implemented. The difference was hard to see, but Julia could feel it, the loss. She could feel the loss of everyone's freedom.

Justin decelerates the sedan to a slow roll, following Julia's hand that is pointing to a dirt road ahead.

Julia pulls a handgun from the glovebox and slides up in her seat, scanning the woods that slowly start to encircle the vehicle as they roll along the brown country road.

"Okay, this is far enough. We should walk from here. Just to be safe. Pull in right there." Julia points to a small break in the trees.

Justin pulls the car in slowly. Branches start scratching along both sides of the car as he edges his way into the light underbrush.

He turns the car off and takes one of the handguns from Julia.

They both begin pushing on their doors a couple of times, back and forth, creating a wide enough opening for them to exit into the brush that now camouflaged the car.

Justin makes his way to the trunk and pulls his rifle out. He begins adjusting the scope.

"Alright, you ready?" Julia asks.

Justin winks an eye.

"Follow me then." Julia says, and begins walking back toward the dirt road they were just driving on.

She takes a knee after a few moments of walking. "Alright, their trailer is less than two clicks from here. And walk slow, I helped them booby trap this whole area with small explosives."

"Got it." Justin takes a knee beside her.

"And lower your weapon if you see them." Julia says, still kneeling.

"How do I know they won't shoot me?"

"Umm, you don't. But if we were Society agents, the brothers would want to keep us alive, initially anyways, to try and extract information from us."

"So, you're saying that we are just more likely to get shot in the leg instead of in the face?"

"Yeah, I guess you could put it like that."

"Great. Sounds like fun." Justin tries to smile and ease his nerves.

"Come on, let's go." Julia starts walking and Justin follows.

"I'm definitely bringing this up to Robert when we get back though. All this planning, but we never had a backup plan to identify ourselves to others that were not TSOMBIEs, or part of The Society?"

Julia looks back and motions for him to stop talking, with a finger on her lips.

"It would be great not to get shot. That's all I'm saying." Justin whispers back.

After creeping through the woods for about fifteen minutes, Julia takes a knee again.

Justin pulls his rifle up, zooming in with the scope on what she is looking at in the distance.

There is a group of trees that are in disarray, busted open and leaning upon another, some on the ground. Blackened and charred by an obvious explosion of some kind.

Julia looks over to Justin, with doubt in her eyes.

They pick up and keep moving forward, slowly.

They observe the first blast site in close detail as they pass it. No bodies. They keep moving forward.

A few hundred meters later and they come upon another site. Same scene. They keep moving forward.

The brother's trailer soon comes into their sight.

Julia spots a body with her naked eye, and then points it out to Justin.

Cautiously, they begin clearing the surrounding area. All clear. There is no presence of anyone else in the woods.

They stop and observe the dead body.

The body is decomposed. Several weeks old by their best guess. But the small frame of the body is a clear identifying sign to Julia, it is of the youngest brother.

Justin taps Julia on the shoulder and points to another body, about fifty feet away.

Julia bends down when they approach the second body and studies over it in detail. It takes her a little longer to differentiate which brother it is, due to the decomposition and size of the body, but she discovers it to be the middle brother.

Justin can tell she is affected by their deaths. He gives her space to grieve on her own while he continues searching carefully around the trailer, expecting to find the third body.

Nothing. No other body is there.

Bullet holes covered the outside of the trailer.

Justin opens the front door that was still halfway hanging on. There is nothing in the front room, but he could smell something dead, and rotting away. He covers his face with his shirt collar and walks down the narrow hallway of the trailer. He clears an open bedroom and small bathroom on the left side of the trailer. Only a thin trailer wall and back door was on his right.

He stands in front of the last room of the trailer, listening to a light humming noise coming from behind the last closed door. He pushes the bedroom door open slowly with the barrel of his rifle. The last brother.

The third body was somewhat on spotlight display, sitting in a chair in the far corner of the room. The fading evening sunlight, spraying through the shattered window and bullet-shredded curtains, shining beautifully on his decaying corpse.

Justin turns his head quickly and swats the formation of flies and gnats from his face. It takes him a minute after they fly away, but then he notices that there is something different about this body. This body was fresher than the other two.

He moves around the bed to get a closer look.

There is a shotgun, leaning slightly on top the bloodstained boot from the floor.

Justin leans in closer and swats away a few of the greedier flies from the oldest brother's face.

One shot to the head, under his chin. Half of his jaw is still hanging on by some blood-dried, stringy muscle tendons. The back half of the skull is peeled open, like a blooming grapefruit flower.

He had taken his own life.

Justin hears something hitting the floor from the front room, and a slight shift of weight from the trailer that is on cement blocks.

"Justin?"

He immediately tosses a bedsheet over the body and moves back around the bed, and then closes the door quickly behind him.

He looks up at Julia from the other end of the hall, and he shakes his head.

"I'm sorry, Julia."

She turns and exits the trailer.

Justin follows her out. His rifle hits the edge of the hanging front door on the way out, knocking it off completely.

Justin catches up to Julia and grabs her arm. "Hey, I'm sorry. It's not your fault, Julia."

"I know." Julia lets out a few deep sighs. "Thanks, Justin. I'll be alright."

She walks over to the middle body and stands over it for a moment.

"It's better for them, this way. They all died together, fighting. None of them had to go on living without one another. They would have chosen to die this way."

Justin just nods.

He did not have the have the heart to tell her the truth about the third brother. It was bad enough they were all dead, and Julia seemed content with the way she thought they all died. It would not do any good to tell her how the oldest brother really died.

"Come on, Justin. There's no need to stay here any longer. Let's get back to the car before it gets dark."

* * *

Robert studies the road map in his car before trying to get a few hours of sleep for the night. He looks in the distance at the bright lights along the highway, Interstate-Forty.

Up to this point, he had been able to avoid all major highways. But now, he would need to travel along the interstate to make it to his next stop in a reasonable amount of time. It would take almost an entire extra day of driving from bypassing the highway, versus just a few hours of driving by taking it. More miles meant more gas. More gas meant more stops for gas. And more stops meant more interactions with TSOMBIEs.

Robert tries to focus on moving forward to the next stop, but images from his first stop keep running through his mind.

His former team member, and one of his oldest friends, left bound to a chair. Single gunshot to his leg. Leaving him to die slowly of blood loss. AGI injection needles on the floor. His corpse was over a month old, Robert guessed, based on the signs of decomposition.

Had he talked? He knew the locations of two other contacts, did he give them up? What info did they get from him? Had the other contacts been killed as well, like this? Robert keeps asking himself these questions, over, and over again.

Robert knew that he needed to stay sharp and focused on the mission at hand. He could compromise everyone if he panicked.

He continues trying to block out the thoughts and tries to just get some rest for the night.

After hours of self-debate, Robert flips the safety on his handgun, leans back in his seat, and closes his eyes.

FIFTEEN

"Okay, thanks for the morning update everyone. Let's get to it then."

Scott looks out into his department, as the analysts leave his office and return to their workstations on the floor. He almost spills his coffee when he sees Mike in the department.

Scott immediately heads over to him. He watches Mike shuffling through papers and through his desk drawers, obviously searching for something.

"Mike. Hey, glad to see you back at work. Where have you been man? You don't answer or return any of my calls. I was beginning to think that you were not coming back."

"Is it okay if I take some of the bloodline files out of my old...out of your office?"

"Umm, yeah. Sure. They're your files anyway. I mean you created them."

"Thanks."

Mike grabs the stack of folders from his desk and walks quickly to Scott's office.

Scott follows quickly behind him. Chris looks at Scott with curiosity. Scott shrugs his shoulders back at him.

Mike tries opening a drawer that's locked, in Scott's office.

"Let me get that for you." Scott leans over and unlocks it.

Mike scatters the files on top of Scott's desk and starts sorting through them.

"Mike. Hey, Mike."

Mike pauses sorting through the files and looks up at Scott.

"You mind telling me what this is all about? I am technically still your boss, you know?"

Mike looks back down at the desk and continues going through the papers.

"Look, I don't care what you do, Mike. But, I still need to know what you are doing. I mean, you're putting me in a bad spot with Tasha and your father by keeping me in the dark."

Mike finds the files he is looking for and packs them in his briefcase, along with the others. He looks at Scott, who is still patiently waiting on a reply.

"I'm going to Kentucky for a few days. For research on the bloodlines in the camp."

Scott looks confused and doesn't know how to respond.

Mike walks to the door. He stops and turn back to Scott, "I'm going to find him."

Scott watches him walk out and exit the department.

Chris comes in Scott's office right afterwards. "What was that all about, sir?"

Scott sits and stares down at the desk for a few moments before responding. He looks up to Chris with wondering eyes, "He's going to search for Rawlings."

SIXTEEN

Walter Rockmann shakes his drink, as he stares out of the private jet window. He watches the Eastern seaboard of the United States slowly begin to appear, just as the plane begins descending. He sips the remainder of his drink, thinking what life will be like after he wins the election.

Walter Rockmann was the logical choice and majority favorite of The Society, to take over for Michael Hardy. The Rockmann family had a very long, and very distinguished, history of wealth and power. They were the primary financier for The Society and TSOMBIE program research, from the very beginning in the late eighteen-hundreds. The Hardy and Rockmann families were, without a doubt, the top two bloodlines within the Inner Circle.

Over the recent years there had always been rumors circulating amongst The Society about

Rockmann taking over. But nothing was ever officially brought up for discussion or votes, mainly out fear and respect, but mostly fear. And generally speaking, all of the bloodlines within the Inner Circle were accustomed to, and very satisfied with, their roles within The Society.

Now, with Phase Three implemented, and controlling the entire world was just a heartbeat away, the desire to be the one family in control of all that power was very appealing.

SEVENTEEN

"There. Good as new." Nichole says, crawling out from behind a washing machine.

"What was it?" Evelyn asks, holding a somewhat large, fluffy white cat in her hands.

"It was nothing, Mom. The power cord was just a little loose."

Her mom leans in closer and whispers, "It was them. They were in here again last night."

"Come on, Mom. It was just a loose cord."

The look of concern on her mother's face does not go away.

"Why would someone sneak in your house, late at night, just to unplug your washing machine? Or rearrange your dishes? Or close your curtains? Or whatever it is you always call me over here for. It doesn't make any sense, Mom. Think about it."

Evelyn thinks for a moment and then seems to settle with Nichole's comments.

"Look, Mom…if you want me to, I can bring some of my things over and stay with you for a while."

Evelyn lets out a light smile and sigh, and then puts her cat down.

"No sweetie, I'll be alright with 'Trixie and Mixie' here with me. I'm sorry to bug you all the time with this stuff. And you're right, I guess it doesn't make much sense for someone to go to all that trouble just to scare an old woman like me. I guess my memory just isn't what it used to be anymore."

They hug each other and then walk to Evelyn's front door.

"Bye, Mom. I'll see you tonight at seven."

Evelyn looks at her, confused.

"Seven. Dinner at Uncle Chad's house. Remember?"

"Right. Right. Oh yes, I remember now."

The cats begin growling and hissing loudly in the other room.

"Mixie! You leave her alone now!" Evelyn begins walking toward the commotion.

"Bye, Mom." Nichole says softly, closing the door quickly behind herself. She can hear her mom yelling at the cats from outside the house. She shakes her head and starts walking back to her house.

Nichole spots a set of feet planted on her porch steps, from around the small bushes in front of her house.

"Lilly? Hey. Is everything alright?"

Li-Li stands and smiles.

"Yeah, yeah. I'm fine. Nothing is wrong or anything."

"Okay. Umm, I mean good. It's good to see you, out and about. Have you been waiting here long?"

"No. Maybe five minutes or so."

"Good. I was just over at my mom's house, helping her with a few things."

"Is she alright? I thought I heard yelling."

"Yeah, she was. She's fine though."

Nichole smiles awkwardly and looks away for a second.

Li-Li starts to smile back, but she sees that Nichole is thinking of something else.

A few seconds go by.

"Well, to be honest, her memory is starting to go. You know, she forgets stuff. And then she gets paranoid a lot. I mean, she thinks that 'they' come into her house and…well, never mind. Sorry. So, anyways, what's going on with you?"

"Look, Nikki, I know that I haven't really talked much to anyone since I have been here…and I…well…I think I'm finally ready for some normal, social interaction again."

Nichole smiles.

"And I'm out of sugar. Your cousin keeps coming by and asking me for a cup, almost every day. He says he ran out."

"Really? Oh my." Nichole laughs softly and shakes her head.

"What's funny about borrowing sugar? I don't get it."

"Well, Brent always has sugar in his house, always. I think-" Nichole stops and smiles.

"What? You think what?"

"I think that maybe he likes you, and he is just trying to find a way to talk to you. He's not really the Casanova-type, if you know what I mean."

Li-Li smiles and laughs softly with Nichole.

"I can beat him up for you if you want? I did it all the time when we were kids."

They both laugh and smile for a minute.

"Well, do you want to go to the store with me? I can finally show you around the base a little bit. We could grab a coffee, or a drink? Or, whatever."

"Yeah. Yes, that would be nice."

"Yeah? Alright then. Let me just go inside for a minute to change my shirt and wash my hands, and then we can go."

Li-Li nods and waits on the porch for Nichole.

Nichole comes back out a few minutes later. "Okay, I'm ready. Oh, wait, I forgot my car keys."

"Do you mind if we just walk? It's really nice outside." Li-Li asks before Nichole enters the house again.

"Umm, yeah. I guess we could walk. It's only a mile or so away to the small shopping center. We would still need to drive if you wanted to go the big shopping center, with all the restaurants and stuff."

"The small one is fine. I just want to stretch my legs and talk."

"Yeah, that does sound nice."

EIGHTEEN

Robert stands in silence, holding a small, toy car in his hand. He puts the toy in his pocket and closes the hatch in the floor, the hatch where he assumes Dr. Nichols' son must have been hiding.

He pauses on the way out of the small shack in the woods and stares at his friend Ian's body, covered in bullet holes, and two handguns on the floor beside him. The bloodstained doorway and entrance to the small, single-bedroom hideaway, was a clear sign that Ian had at least taken out one of them as they entered.

But Kenton was gone.

Robert punches the plywood wall out of anger, thinking of the promise he made to his friend, Dr. Nichols. A promise that he was unable to keep.

Robert lets out a deep breath and regains his composure. He leaves the shack and begins making his way back through the woods and down the small mountain, focusing on his next stop.

* * *

"Justin. Justin. Hey, wake up!"

Justin removes the shirt from his face and squints as his eyes adjust to the strong, afternoon sunlight. He raises the passenger seat forward.

"Mm…what is it?" Justin moans and grabs his sunglasses from the dash.

"I think we are being followed."

"Huh? What are you talking about?" Justin looks quickly in the sideview mirror but doesn't see anything. He turns to look out of the back window.

"I don't see anyone. There's nothing back there, Julia."

Julia eases off the accelerator and slows down, about ten miles per hour slower.

"Just wait a minute. Keep watching and just wait a minute."

Justin looks at Julia and then at the speedometer, and then he looks out of the back window again, waiting.

"I was sleeping good too," Justin mumbles softly, looking out of the window still.

About one minute goes by.

He shakes his head and begins turning back around in his seat.

"Alright. Ha-ha, you got me, Julia. I'm going back to sleep now."

Julia reaches out and keeps him from turning all the way back around.

Justin feels her grip on him and looks at her face. He sees that she is serious.

"Keep watching."

Less than another minute goes by and Justin sees something. A tiny reflection of sunlight hitting something on the road, far behind them.

"There," Julia says calmly. "You see it now?"

Justin keeps watching and can barely make out the description of the vehicle before it fades out of sight again.

"Yeah, I see a van, I think. So, what? We've seen over ten vans on these roads out here. I mean, how do you know 'that' van is following us?"

"When I slow down, so does that van. If it was a TSOMBIE driving the van, then they would have kept the speed limit pace and passed us already. I have slowed down and sped up three times already before I woke you up. And I saw the van back in Missouri, I think."

"It's just a white van, Julia. How do you know it is the same one?"

"Why would they be changing speeds like that then? Justin? Slowing down...or speeding up...after I do? Staying just within sight of us?"

Justin realizes that she has a point.

"We are too isolated out here on these back roads. It's too easy for someone to keep track of us."

Julia looks over at Justin, "So, what are you thinking then?"

"We need to get off this highway and get to a city. We can lose them easier in a crowded area. And then we can get back on our mission, or go back in. But either way, we need to lose them first."

Justin pulls a map out and looks at his watch. He begins doing quick math in his head and circles a city on the map. He holds it over the console and points out the city to Julia.

"What do you think?"

Julia nods in approval.

"Alright, we can make it there in under an hour if we jump on the interstate up here. And make sure your face is straight before we start passing through all of the cameras."

Justin puts the map up and pulls out two Phase Three flu shots from his backpack. He injects himself in the arm.

Julia holds the steering wheel with her left hand and extends her right arm to Justin. He injects her.

They both look at each other with trust and confidence, and then they focus on the road ahead.

Julia changes lanes a few miles later and shifts to the highway onramp, as the interstate sign to Colorado Springs appears overhead.

* * *

Julia and Justin stare ahead in disciplined silence, carefully observing the crowded downtown scene that they were now driving through.

They stop at a red light.

Julia looks in the rear-view mirror. "There are too many cars now. I can't tell if the van is still back there or not."

Justin looks in the sideview mirror. He sees a few drops of rain hit the mirror as he makes out the van, several cars behind them. "I see it."

He looks forward and begins mapping out a plan in his head.

Julia turns on the windshield wipers as a soft and steady rain begins.

The light turns green.

Justin points across the four-way intersection at another white van. "Wait, there's another van right there, on that side street."

Julia glances at the van and then back to the road, and she notices a car pulling off from the row of parked cars on the street. She quickly and instinctively takes the empty parking spot.

"What are you doing? What are we parking for?" Justin asks, somewhat confused.

Julia watches one van passes by them and continues straight.

Justin looks at Julia and sees her staring in the sideview mirror. He looks in the rear-view mirror and watches the second van turn onto the street that they were now parked on.

They both watch as the van slowly drives past them. They slide into their seats a little deeper and read the graphics on the side of the van as it passes, 'ANN – American News Network.'

"What's happening? I can't see it anymore. What's it doing?" Justin asks, unable to see due to the rain and large SUV parked in front of them.

"It just parked." Julia says, and begins sliding her seat back a little.

"Why would a news van be following us? Are you sure it is the same one?"

"Maybe. Maybe not."

Julia pulls her handgun from under the seat and places it in her jacket. She pulls the hood over her head and looks over at Justin.

"But I'm going to that coffee shop right there to take a closer look and find out."

"What? Wait…" Justin shakes his head at the idea.

"We need to know who this is, Justin. We can't go back to the bunker, or to any other contact locations, if Society agents are following us. We need to know, and we need to deal with it, now."

Julia looks in the vanity mirror of the sun visor and gently rubs the fake, dark facial hair around her mouth and chin.

Justin wants to talk her out of it and tell her to think of a different plan, but he is speechless.

The wiper blades thump in a slight, offbeat rhythm on the windshield.

Julia looks at Justin and knows that he is trying to think of a different plan. She takes a deep breath and lets it out as she opens the door. She looks back at Justin.

"Alright. Wish me luck."

"What if it is the Society? What then?"

Julia wipes the rain from her brow.

"Then this is it. This is what we trained for, Justin. Weren't you the one complaining about being stuck in the bunker with nothing to do? Well, here is something to do." Julia smiles and wipes the rain from her brow again.

"This is not…"

Julia slams the door and enters the crosswalk towards the coffee shop.

"…what I had in mind."

Justin slides over the center console and into the driver seat. He gets a quick look at the van, blurred by the rain. He keeps one hand on the steering wheel and one on the gear shift. And he waits.

Julia tries to get a glimpse of the driver in the van, but the door of the coffee shop opens, and a woman exits and brushes her shoulder.

Julia removes her hood and enters the coffee shop. She moves slowly towards the counter and stands in the small line of average, normal-looking people.

She scans the store with her peripherals and realizes that nobody is paying attention to her. The customers sitting at the tables are glued to their phones. The only conversations going on are between the workers and people placing their orders. There doesn't appear to be any uninfected present, other than her. It is safe. They are all TSOMBIEs.

Julia had been in this coffee chain store before, before all of this started over two years ago. Now that she was thinking about it, this was really the only coffee shop chain around now. However, the menu was noticeably shorter now. Coffee. Water. Muffin.

Julia moves up in the line and watches the man in front of her stick his index finger in the rapid scanner. A light blinks green on the machine after a few seconds. He then orders and pays with a credit card.

Julia moves forward and places her finger in the scanner. She takes a slow breath and after a few seconds, the light blinks, green. No pin prick though. These scanners must be checking body temperature only, she thinks to herself. They looked like the other scanners that Nichols designed, just a little smaller.

"Hello, sir." The young man behind the counter says to Julia.

"May I take your order?"

Julia pauses before ordering as she realizes that something is wrong, different. Something is missing. No cash register.

"Sir, may I take your order?" The young man asks again, in the same monotone voice.

Julia improvises and pulls out her phone.

"Hello? Okay. I will wait for you." She says in a slow, deep voice.

Julia puts the phone back in her jacket and looks at the employee behind the counter.

"I'm sorry. I need to wait for someone."

"Of course, sir. Next in line please."

Julia steps aside and moves slowly to a table by the window, in good view of the van. She looks across the street and tries to see Justin, but the rain is too thick now. She can just make out the car through the downpour.

She looks back at the van and squints through the crowd of people and umbrellas on the sidewalk. The driver door opens and closes. She catches a glimpse of a man in a dark coat and ball cap, getting out of the van.

Julia pulls her phone out again, this time to call Justin. She notices the CCTV camera in the corner that is facing in her direction.

She hangs up the phone and slowly exits the shop. She pulls the hood back up on her jacket and begins following the driver of the van.

"Hello? Julia?" Justin says into his phone. He looks across the street at the coffee shop and sea of umbrellas on the sidewalk. It is all one big blur through the rain. He tries calling Julia back, but the phone just rings. He hangs up and waits anxiously.

"I knew this was a bad idea." Justin says to himself.

He pulls his handgun out and checks the chamber.

"Come on, Julia."

A short siren whale from behind the car startles Justin. He sees blue lights in the rear-view mirror.

Julia stops at the next intersection and crosswalk, up the street from the van. She scans around in all directions, trying to locate the man again. She spots him, across the street. She begins to cross but the light flashes red and vehicle traffic begins moving again.

Julia pulls her phone out and calls Justin again. The phone just rings, no answer.

"Come on, Justin. Pick up."

Justin watches as the police officer exits the patrol car and approaches his vehicle window. He carefully slides his gun under his legs in the seat and then closes them, placing his wallet in his lap, above the concealed gun.

The officer bends down at the window.

"Please roll down your window, sir."

Justin knew what the officer said, even though his voice was being drowned out by the rain.

He rolls the window down halfway. Water begins splashing wildly and sporadic into the car.

"Sir, you have not paid to park here. Please give me your license or identification card."

Justin's eyes automatically blink from a few drops of rain splashing in his face.

The officer repeats himself in a robotic tone, "Sir, please give me your license or identification card."

Justin lets out a deep breath and begins moving his right hand slowly toward his wallet, gently opening his legs and closing his eyes.

The officer stands up straight and says something.

Justin opens his eyes to the muffled voice, with his hand now wrapped around the pistol grip between his legs. He looks up at the officer's waistline in the window and can hear a faint conversation over the windshield wipers and the rain.

There is a conversation over the roof of the car between the officer and some other man that was standing on the passenger side of the car. Justin's eyes go back and forth between the two men, and then he cracks the passenger side window in an attempt to better make out what they are saying.

"…nice day sir." The unknown man on the passenger side says.

The police officer begins walking back to his patrol car.

Justin sits and watches in confusion, still gripping the pistol. He looks through the windshield at the man who was just talking to the cop. He watches him swipe a credit card through the parking meter scanner and then drops the card on the ground, intentionally.

The parking meter lights up like the rest on the street, and the blue lights turn off as the police car drives away.

"Hey!" The man yells through the small crack in the passenger window at Justin. "Open the door man!"

Justin adjusts his grip on the gun and rolls down the window a little further, enough for him to look at the man's face.

The door handle shakes on the outside of the car.

"Come on man, I just saved your life right there." He says, wiping the rain from his face and noticing the slight sheen of the gun in Justin's hand.

"Look bro, if I wanted to hurt you I could have done that hundreds of miles ago, in the middle of nowhere, not here in a crowded city with cameras everywhere. I'm not with them. Come on, I'm getting soaked out here man. Let me in."

Justin thinks about what the man just said, and he assumes that he must be the one that has been following them. Hundreds of miles ago, Justin thinks to himself. Justin unlocks the door.

As soon as the man sits down and closes the door, Justin jams his gun into his ribs.

"Is that really necessary? I'm just trying to help."

"Yes, it is really necessary. Now, empty your pockets. Slowly."

The man complies and carefully empties his pockets, placing the contents in his lap.

Justin observes the items, nothing of importance or dangerous. Justin changes hands with the gun and pats the man down with his free hand. Justin finishes the frisk search and sits back in his seat, his gun still pointed at the man.

"Can you please put the gun away now? You already searched me, and I don't have any weapons on me. I don't really do the whole weapons thing."

"Who are you? And have you been following us?"

"You might know me as DJ Paris? I have a couple of mixed tapes out, pretty big in the club scene. Well…I mean I used to be…before all of this started anyways."

Justin smirks.

"Nope. I never heard of you. And I've never been into the whole 'club' thing. Now, have you been following us?" Justin points the gun closer to him.

"Yes. Yes. And I will tell you why, okay. I promise. But we need to get out of here first. You and your sister are about to draw a lot of unnecessary attention."

"My sister? How do you know…"

The rear passenger door opens, and Julia gets in quickly, immediately pressing her handgun hard into the passenger seat. She removes her hood and looks at Justin with wide eyes.

"What the hell is he doing in here? This is the guy from the van that has been following us."

The man begins to turn around to Julia, "Hi, I'm…"

"Face forward! Don't look at me!" Julia says, pointing the weapon at his head.

The man quickly faces forward again.

Julia begins frisking the man, over the seat with her free hand.

"I've already searched him. He's clean."

"Umm…I hate to interrupt here, but if both of you are going to shoot me for trying to help you, then may I just suggest that you do it somewhere else, instead of in a crowded city. That meter over there only has about ten minutes left on it, and that cop might come back."

Julia nods to Justin. Justin puts his gun away and begins driving.

"Can you stop at my van? I want to get my tapes and stuff."

"Keep driving," Julia says.

"Okay, I guess not then." The man says, as they drive past it.

Julia pokes the back of the man's seat with the barrel of her gun.

"And you, keep quiet until we tell you to talk."

Justin glances in the rear-view at Julia and then keeps driving, out of the city.

NINETEEN

Richard walks into a small office and sees Michael Hardy, Junior, sitting in a chair.

The guards escort Richard in and close the door.

"Have a seat, Richard."

Richard sits down, across the table from Mike, and clears his throat as he looks at the guards posted by the door.

"Do you know who I am?"

"Yes, sir. You're Michael Hardy, and your father runs The Society."

Mike nods and begins looking through a stack of papers in front of him on the table.

"I have been reading through all of your reports, Richard, and everyone in The Society thinks that you are really doing a great job here."

"I just do what I am told, sir. No more, no less."

Mike nods again.

"I see. Well, do you know why I am here, Richard?"

"No, I do not." Richard adjusts himself in his seat and looks at the guards again.

Mike slides a photo of Robert Rawlings across the small table to Richard.

"Robert Rawlings? I'm still not sure that I understand, Mr. Hardy."

"I need to find him, Richard. Wait, let me rephrase that. I am going to find him. This little game of hide and seek has gone on long enough. And that is why I am here. Because I find it hard to believe that nobody here, not a single person, knows anything about where Robert Rawlings might be."

"Mr. Hardy, sir, we have all been through multiple interviews and we were all questioned about Rawlings before. Several times, sir."

"Well, that as it may be, I still think something might have been overlooked. Maybe something that the field agents just didn't pick up on. Something small and benign that didn't seem important at the time. Again, this is why I am here. I am going to talk to everyone again, personally. I am going to ensure that nothing was, in fact, overlooked. So, I will expect the utmost cooperation from everyone here. Do you understand what I am saying, Richard?"

Richard nods quietly.

"Good. The others in your community are being brought here as we speak. So, while we are waiting for them, let's just go ahead and start with you."

Mike pulls a small, personal video recorder out of his briefcase and turns it on.

"And remember, Richard, no detail is too small not to mention."

Richard looks at the camera and nods silently again.

"Okay then, let's begin."

* * *

Richard walks into the newcomer briefing room, now filled with all of the other non-Society bloodlines from the camp. He wipes the sweat from his forehead and makes eye contact with Nichole. He quickly breaks eye contact with her and begins walking to the coffee machine in the corner of the room.

Nichole makes her way to the coffee machine. "Richard. Hey, what's going on? I heard someone important and high-up from The Society is here."

Richard stirs a little sugar into his coffee.

"Yeah, you heard right. Hardy himself. The son."

"Really? Why?"

Richard takes a sip of coffee and looks out into the room.

"He's on a personal mission to find Rawlings. And he thinks something might have been missed on the previous interviews here."

"Interviews? Those were interrogations we went through. Come on, Richard."

Nichole refills her cup with coffee. She motions no at the offering of sugar from Richard.

She takes a small drink and lowers her voice as she continues talking. "I mean, they know the intimate details of my menstrual cycle for crying out loud. What could they have possibly 'missed' in our previous, so-called interviews?"

"Nikki, please."

"Well, it's the truth and you know it. They interrogated us."

They look at each other in silence and take another drink.

"Why now though? I mean, it's been months since the bombings against them." Julia asks, staring back out into the room.

Richard refills his cup. He looks at Nichole, deep in her thoughts.

He changes the subject, "How's everyone doing?"

"Fine, I guess. Curious. Same as me."

"And Lilly? How is she coming along? I saw you guys walking past my house the other day."

"Yeah, she's doing better. She's finally starting to open up a little. And I finally showed her around the base a little bit, that day you saw us walking. And, she told me what happened to her brother."

"Really? Wow, she is opening up then. What else?"

"Calm down, Richard. You've got that 'Wild Brent' look of curiosity in your eyes."

Richard shakes his head at the remark, smiling just a little and then goes back to being serious. He looks at one of the cameras in the room and then brings his cup near his mouth, covering his lips as he continues their conversation.

"I know what is on everyone's mind around here. And well, I would be lying if I said I didn't feel the same way."

Nichole looks at him talking into his cup and follows his lead. "And what way is that, Richard?"

"Hopeful. Hopeful that there may be more 'of' us out there. And hopeful that there may be more 'for' us out there."

"Wow," Nichole says in a sarcastic, dull tone. "Getting tired of brown-nosing, Richard?"

"Look, Nikki." He catches himself raising his voice and then lowers it back down.

"Look, I know what you guys think of me. That I am a sellout. That I am helping them."

"Well, I'm not sure I would put it like that. But yeah, I guess that pretty much sums it up."

Richard stares at her hard for the interruption and then he continues.

"Here's the truth. I am just doing whatever it takes to keep us all safe. Whatever it takes to keep 'them' from having any reason not to trust me anymore. I do everything for all of you, not for me. I have no family left. You guys are all the…forget it. You know, did you ever stop and think for one second that I might know what I'm doing, that I might have a plan?"

Nichole looks at him and can see the genuine conviction in his eyes. The truth. She puts down her cup and looks back into his eyes.

"Okay, Richard. Okay. Then why the sudden change to tell me all of this? After all this time of being here?"

"Because Lilly brings us hope now...but Hardy, Hardy doesn't. If he does catch Rawlings, then the hope that Lilly has brought will be gone. That would crush everyone's will to ever think about escaping."

A guard comes out of the interview office and points to someone in the front row.

"We shouldn't talk anymore about this, here. Tomorrow. Water fountain. You, me, and Lilly. And tell her to bring her drawings that she always carries around."

Richard tosses his cup in the trash and walks off.

Nichole refills her coffee and watches on, as Richard makes his way around the room, conversing in small-talk with everyone from the camp.

Nichole takes another drink and looks at Lilly, drawing with Kenton. She watches them talk and smile as they draw.

And she feels it. Richard was right. Lilly gave them hope.

*   *   *

"Okay, we are here. So, now can you tell me why we had to come here to talk? I don't understand how this is safe. We are out in the open and there are cameras literally everywhere."

Li-Li sits down beside Nichole on the water fountain wall and waits for an answer to her question.

Nichole swishes her hand in the water and shakes it off.

"The running water distorts the audio too much. Just don't look straight at a camera when you do talk, so they can't try to read your lips. We've tested it out before, and they can't make out what we are saying here. We are sure they know about it the deficiency, but they haven't bothered fixing the audio capability or shutting down the fountain. And we haven't given them any reason to yet."

Richard walks up, and acts surprised to see them.

"Alright. I'm going to sit down beside you Lilly, and then you are going to pass me your drawings. That is what we will act like we are talking about. Understood?"

Li-Li nods.

"Good."

Richard sits down and Li-Li hands him the drawings. He begins running his hands over the pages and holding them up, appearing to study them in detail.

"Okay Nichole, keep time. We need to stick to five minutes or less. I'll get right to the point, Lilly. You lasted months longer out there than any of us. We need you to teach us how you did it."

Richard looks at her and then holds another drawing out in front of him.

"After that, after you teach us, it will be up to you if you want to leave with us. Or, stay in here. The same choice we all will have to make when the time comes. But in any case, nobody that leaves will stand a chance out there without your knowledge on how to survive undetected."

Richard pauses and flips the pages to another drawing.

"Okay. After I do it, after I help train you, what then? How are you going to get out of here in the first place? This place is almost like a fortress around the perimeter walls. Do you even have a plan on how to escape yet?"

"Yes. Well, sort of."

"And? What is it?"

"Well, I don't know how solid the info is, but supposedly there is an underground network of tunnels under this base that extend several miles outside the perimeter. There are rumors that they were used a long time ago to smuggle gold out of here."

"Don't tell me you are basing your plan, our plan of escaping, off Brent's crazy war stories? Really?"

Richard puts down the drawing and glares at Nichole for interrupting.

"Sorry. Two minutes left." Nichole says somewhat apologetic, trying to eradicate her last sentiment of sheer doubt.

"Why leave? It is the same in here as it is out there now. Plus, we are all safer in here. Why…"

"Because…because it's not 'our' life in here. It is the life they are making us live. They took our freedom."

Richard breaks eye contact with Li-Li and focuses back on the drawings.

"So, you want to run? And hide? For the rest of your life? Always looking over your shoulder? What kind of life is that?"

Richard looks her in the eyes again and snaps back. "It would be mine. My life. My choice."

He looks down at the ground for a few long seconds.

"I'm sorry. It may not be as cozy out there as it is in here, or as easy, but it would be my life out there, mine. But I can't make it out there without your help. None of us can."

Li-Li looks at Richard, and then at Nichole. She feels it. She understands how they see her now, as a source of inspiration, hope. Hope to survive. Hope to live. She understands.

"Okay. If I do this, if I help you, how many people do you think will join you and escape? Everyone?"

"No, not everyone. For some it won't even be physically possible, and then, there will probably be some that will choose to stay. But, we will still need everyone to help with the escape, to created diversions and serve as lookouts, to give us our best chance."

"A minute left." Nichole says.

"Okay. Yes, I'll do it. I will help you."

Richard smiles at Li-Li and hands her the drawings back after he stands up.

"Nikki, meet here and at the other dead spot with small groups of all the females over the next few days. I'll do the same with the men. The three of us will meet back here after that, to confirm who is leaving, and who is staying. Then, we will go from there with the planning."

Richard looks back at Li-Li, "Thank you."

Richard waves bye to them and they all walk away from each other in separate directions.

A guard approaches Richard as he gets in his car. Richard rolls down the window and takes a deep breath.

"Yes?"

"Mr. Hardy would like to speak with you before he leaves the base, sir. Please come with me."

TWENTY

"Thank you everyone for the updates," Tasha says, standing with the room full of AGI leaders and placing their hands over their hearts for a few seconds.

"Scott." Tasha says, motioning with her head for him to follow her.

Scott shakes hands with a couple of members in the room as he follows Tasha out.

They enter Tasha's office and take seats.

Tasha lights a cigarette and leans back in her chair. "So. Is the mental case back from his little trip yet?"

"Umm, he should be back later today."

Tasha exhales a small cloud of smoke. "I can't believe he is doing this. He is only going to make us all look bad when he doesn't find Rawlings, again."

Scott tilts his head slightly and Tasha sees that he might not agree with her.

"What? Oh, come on, Scott. You do not actually think that Mike is going to find him? Do you?"

"No. I don't know, but…"

"But what?"

"Well, he seemed really determined when he told me about it. I mean, I have seen him focused before when he was working the Rawlings case before, but this…well, this was different. It was like, finding him was his sole purpose in life, and nothing else mattered, I mean absolutely nothing else."

"Yeah? Well, he's still batting goose eggs when it comes to finding Rawlings. So, just keep close tabs on him from now on. And let's keep his extracurricular activities as quiet as we can for the time being. I do not want word about this personal hunt of his getting out. All we need is for the other candidates to hear about this and they start using it against us in their election campaigns to sway the other voters."

"Understood."

Tasha puts the cigarette out and smiles at Scott, signaling the meeting was over.

Scott stands and begins to leave the office.

"And remember Scott, we're moving to the new headquarters soon. Make sure your department is prepped and ready to go. I don't want any gaps in our surveillance coverage or operations because of the move."

Scott nods as he closes the door.

Scott returns to his department and conducts his daily targeting and surveillance meeting with his subordinate supervisors and project leads.

Halfway through the meeting, Scott's concentration is broken as he notices Mike walk through the department doors.

"Umm, Chris, take the rest of the brief please."

"Yes, sir."

Chris stands up and watches Scott walk into the department. He sees Mike at his workstation.

The others sitting at the table all turn around systematically, to take a look as well.

"Mike. Hey. I didn't expect to see you back at work today."

Mike acknowledges his comment without saying anything, and then continues unloading files from his bag to his desk.

"So, did you find out anything new, or useful, while you were down there?"

Mike places the last file down on the stack of folders and turns in his chair to face Scott.

"No, not really. But, I feel better knowing that I personally talked with every one of them. There are a couple of them that seem to be hiding something, but I don't think that it's related to Rawlings. There's not enough there to start doing unorthodox interrogations though, not yet anyways."

"Well, that's some good news. I mean, it's something anyways. Good job, Mike. That kind of information is always good for us to know. We'll tighten up surveillance on them and see if anything comes up that could help you. Us, help us."

Mike leans forward and shakes his head gently.

"Mike? Is something wrong?"

"There has got to be something here that I am just not seeing. Something that I overlooked."

"Mike, you have done more than anyone here on trying to find Rawlings. More than anyone. Why don't you take a few days off again? To relax? You look pretty stressed right now, and that stress is only going to make it harder for you to see things more clearly. Take a few days, take a week. Then you can get back at finding him with a fresh and clear head."

"Yeah, maybe you're right."

Mike starts packing the files back in his bag and stands up.

"Call me if anything new comes up from the bloodline camp."

"You got it. Take care, Mike."

Mike gives him less than a smile and walks away.

"Did he find anything?" Chris asks, startling Scott.

Scott moves away and looks at Chris with hard eyes.

"No."

"I knew it. Man, he's losing it. Good call by sending him home, sir."

Scott smirks at the comment.

"Shouldn't you be typing up my morning report or something? Get back to work, Chris."

"Yes, sir."

Scott turns back around, and watches Mike walk out of the exit doors, with his head draping down and looking defeated, once again.

TWENTY-ONE

Dave opens his eyes to a blinking red light penetrating through the door curtains. He looks over at Amy, sleeping, with Samantha curled up on her side of the small bed. He walks to operations room and turns off the silent alarm light. He then takes a seat behind the computer and pulls up the CCTV camera footage on the monitor.

Nothing.

He starts rewinding the camera footage, not knowing how long the silent alarm light had been going off before it woke him up.

He rewinds the hatch camera footage first. Nothing. He rewinds the tunnel camera footage next. After the footage rolls back ten minutes prior to him waking up, he hits pause. Justin and Julia. He presses play and then pause again. He leans in and looks closer at the image of a third person, a man. And it is not Robert.

"What the…?" Dave says out loud to himself.

"Babe?"

"Woo!" Dave breaths out heavy and almost jumps out of his chair.

"Shh. It's just me."

"You scared the hell out of me."

"Sorry," Amy says, smiling and placing her hand on Dave's shoulder.

She leans over him and looks at the monitor.

"What are you doing? What's going on?"

"I'm not sure yet. Justin and Julia are back a few days early though, and it looks like they found a contact."

"That's good news then, right?"

"Yeah. Good news." Dave pats his wife's hand and looks at the image of the man again.

"Go back to sleep, honey. I'll stay up for them. It will be well over an hour before they get here. They just entered the tunnel about ten to fifteen minutes ago."

"Are you sure? I can stay up with you, if you want?"

"No, I'm okay."

Amy kisses Dave's forehead and disappears through the dimly lit kitchen and into the dark bedroom.

* * *

Dave turns off the handheld game at the familiar sound of the tunnel wall of the bunker sliding open. He gets up from the kitchen table and pours another cup of coffee. He turns around and waits for them.

Julia enters the kitchen first, guiding the unknown man beside her. She shakes her head in mild exhaustion to Dave, and then pulls a chair out from the table.

"Sit down," Julia tells the man, and somewhat pushes him down into the seat. "And keep your hands on the table."

Dave looks at the man with deep curiosity. Bound hands, taped mouth, and blindfolded.

The man wiggles his hands and mumbles something under the tape that is covering his mouth. His hands are bound together and then to his belt loop, preventing him from being able to fully place them on the table.

Julia pulls out her knife and cuts the zip tie connected to his pants.

Justin enters the kitchen and drops his backpack softly on the ground. He begins stretching his neck and back.

"Dave."

"Justin."

Julia takes off her backpack and jacket. She reaches for the cabinet and pulls out the nearly empty, bottle of liquor.

Justin sees his game on the table. He looks at Dave and then picks it up and un-pauses it.

"Ah, come on, Dave. Half of my points are gone now, man."

Julia pours a little bit of coffee into her cup, followed by a small shot of whiskey.

Dave tries to wait calmly for an explanation of what is going on, and for them to tell him who this man is and why he is there. And why he is tied and taped up. But the nearly two hours of waiting for them to walk through the tunnel is wearing his patience thin.

Julia takes a seat and takes a drink. She starts to massage her own neck and stretches in her chair.

Justin reaches over and takes a drink from her cup and then continues playing the game.

Dave's patience finally gives. He takes the bottle of whiskey and puts it on the counter behind them and then slams his hand down on the kitchen table.

Justin and Julia stop what they are doing and look at him. Justin turns off the game and Julia puts down her cup, knowing why Dave did it.

Dave points with an open hand at the man, "Can we please talk about 'this' for a minute?"

"I'm sorry, Dave. It's been a long few days and it was a rough drive back." Julia says.

"Yeah, sorry." Justin says.

Dave lets out a small sigh, knowing he overreacted a little bit. He takes a seat.

"No, no need to apologize guys. I can only imagine what it was like out there."

Dave smiles and they accept the sympathy.

"So, who is this guy? I'm assuming he is not one of our contacts by the zip-ties and blindfold. And why is his mouth taped up?"

The man turns his head toward Dave's general direction, and then he starts mumbling something under the tape and moving his head around like he is talking to him.

Julia kicks the man's chair in a mild manner, almost playful. But the man takes it seriously and he stops making noise.

"Well, he claims to be part of one of the anti-immunization groups. And that is why he's not infected, because he never received the flu shots. We picked him up in Colorado after we realized that he was following us." Justin pauses and looks at the man.

The man mumbles something again and Julia kicks his chair again, and then he stops.

"And, he helped me out of a little situation. He kept me from possibly getting identified by a cop that was trying to write me a ticket, or worse."

The man makes two distinct mumbles under the tape and then shifts in his seat, anticipating Julia's kick.

But she doesn't kick the chair this time. She almost smiles at his non-aggressive and innocent persistence.

"He said there are others in the anti-immunization groups that are still alive and safe out there, hiding. Like us." Julia says.

"How many?" Dave asks.

"He said there are hundreds, maybe more." Justin replies.

The man moves his head up and down, signaling he agrees with Justin's remark, and he does not mumble anything this time.

Dave looks to Julia. She tilts her head sideways and shrugs her shoulders as if she isn't sure if she believes it or not.

"And the contacts?" Dave changes the topic.

Justin looks away.

Julia shakes her head no and then looks down at the table.

Justin gets up and grabs the whiskey bottle, back from the counter that Dave had placed it on. He sits down and takes a small drink. He offers the bottle to Dave.

Dave accepts, closing his eyes and taking a slow sip.

The man wiggles his nose, obviously picking up the scent of the alcohol aroma from beside him.

Dave looks at the man, feeling somewhat sorry for him.

"Why did you tape his mouth? I understand the blindfold and zip-ties, but his mouth?"

"He would not shut up," Julia answers.

"Yeah, he was driving us crazy on the way back," Justin chimes in.

"Well, now that you have brought him here, and we know a little bit about him. And he did help you out there…so, does he still pose any type of threat to us now?

Julia looks at Dave and then at the man.

"Can we trust him enough to at least untie him? I mean, there's really no place for him to go down here. And well, he doesn't have enough weight on him to hurt any of us."

Dave looks over the man again. A little taller than average and a light build. Thin but not boney. Clean-shaven beard and nice, silky brown hair. Handsome face from what could be seen, aside from what the blindfold and tape covered up. Dave guesses he is in his mid to late twenties, probably somewhere between Julia and Justin's age.

Julia and Justin look at each other and contemplate cutting him loose. They nod in agreeance after a few seconds of silent eye-talk.

Julia gives Dave the approval.

Dave gets up and removes the cut-shirt blindfold first.

The man blinks a few times at Dave, his hazel eyes adjusting to light again. He looks around the room at everyone, and then continues scanning around the room.

Dave flips open his knife.

The man looks at the knife and then up at Dave.

Dave cuts off the zip-ties from his hands first. The man immediately reaches to pull the tape off his mouth and Dave catches his hand and then points to his bedroom.

"My wife, and kid, are in there sleeping. So, keep your voice down. Understand?"

He nods, and Dave lets go of his hand. The man pulls the tape off carefully, flexing his jaw after he removes it. After a few seconds of feeling the missing hair around his lips, he looks around at everyone looking back at him.

Dave grabs the bottle and offers it to him.

The man looks at all of them, with uncertainty about what to do.

Dave motions again with bottle. "It's okay. Take it."

He accepts the bottle and takes a small drink, and then tries to control a light series of coughs.

Everyone lets out a slight smile and the tension in the room eases a little bit.

"Thank you...Dave?"

"Yeah, Dave. And you are?"

The man spills a little bit of whiskey from taking another drink and lets out another light cough.

"Umm, my name is DJ. DJ Paris. But, people just call me DJ."

"DJ Paris? What kind of name is that?"

"Well, I'm a music DJ. I was, I mean. I was a radio and club DJ in LA. Techno music mainly."

"Alright, DJ. Let's hear about you and this group you are a part of."

"Yeah, sure. Umm, I'm not exactly sure where to start."

Julia reaches over and grabs the bottle from him.

"Let's start with you," Julia says. "What is your name?"

"But I already told you guys my name, DJ…"

"No, your real name," Julia cuts him off. "Who are you, really?"

There is a moment of silence and tension begins building in the room again.

Justin pulls out a roll of tape from his bag on the floor and places it on the table.

Julia looks at him and shakes her head no, with disapproval.

"Okay. Okay. There's no need for the tape again." DJ says, looking around at everyone, and then stopping at Julia.

"My real name is, Frank…Francis. Francis Alvarez." He looks down at the table.

"Alvarez?" Dave asks, confused.

"Francis?" Justin laughs out and puts the tape back in his bag. "I get it now, Paris, France, Francis. Good one. Real clever." Justin laughs again.

DJ looks down at the table, somewhat embarrassed.

"Go ahead, continue," Julia says.

"I was adopted. Alvarez is my adopted last name. The state, the foster home, gave me my first name. I never knew my real last name."

Justin's smile fades away.

"Keep going," Julia says.

"I never knew my real parents. I grew up under control of the state, bouncing in and out of foster homes until I was finally adopted, at around age eleven. The couple that adopted me were pretty old, and they could not have kids. But they were nice, and they always treated me good. And, they had money, a lot. But I never had a lot of friends growing up. I was really a nerd growing up in high school. And being the anti-social youth that I was, I got pretty serious into computers and electronics. And the couple that adopted me always bought me the best and most expensive hardware to play with. But anyways, the couple…well, they both died while I was in my last year of college. The doctors said it was from the flu. But that year, the same thing happened to some of the kids on campus.

They just killed over. And they were young and healthy. And then some rumors started going around about the government, and the flu shots. Some people were saying that it was the flu shots killing people, and not the flu itself. I was still young, you know. In college, free thinking, etcetera. I was also upset...angry...scared. So, I dropped out of school and joined this small group that a couple of friends of mine were in. It started out with just a few members, typical anti-government type college kids, and some conspiracy nerds. Pretty small, you know. But then, the group started to grow over the next couple of months and word spread fast. We were starting to make a name for ourselves with our protests and radio broadcasts, and our public protests started hitting the news. We branched out into other states, even as far wide as New York. We called ourselves, AIM, Anti-Immunization Movement."

DJ pauses and looks around to see if the others recognize the name, and they all look at each other and then back to him. They all lean in more attentive as if they have heard the name before. He continues.

"Then, two years ago, people within our group just started disappearing. And, some of them seemed to just change their beliefs overnight, and then they tried to convince others within the group to get the flu shots. It became hard to tell who could really be trusted after that. So, those of us that were still committed to our cause realized that we needed to split up and go underground. Figuratively, not literally like this. Well, some of them might have, but definitely off the grid is what I mean. So, for me, well I basically started hiding out after that, moving around from one place to another. And at first, it wasn't that hard. But then, everything seemed to change, all at once and without warning. It was right around the flu season this past year and the same time as all of the bombings of The Society buildings and AGI facilities."

He pauses and looks at Justin and Julia for a few seconds.

"After that it became really hard and extremely dangerous to move around anymore. So, I bunkered down, no pun intended, where I was staying at the time. Missouri. And that is where I first saw you two. At the Holland brothers' hideout."

"Wait. You knew them? How?" Justin asks.

Julia leans forward, more intrigued by the last remark.

"One of the leaders of our group reached out to me right after the bombings, and before we lost good contact with each other. He told me that he had linked up with friends from this other type of group. And he said that they were involved with the bombings, and they were connected to Dr. Singer, I mean Rawlings...and you guys of course. Anyways, he told me I should do the same because the government, The Society, was coming after us and other anti-immunization groups too. Even though we were not involved with the bombings, we still posed a threat to what they were doing. My friend told me this group of yours, your father's, had weapons and training, and they could offer us protection. And then, well I just got lucky really. The Holland's hideaway was not impossible to walk to from where I was hiding out at the time. And I had already ditched my car. It ended up being a two-day hike away, through a National Park. And they took me in when I arrived. And then a couple of months went by, and…well…you saw what happened to them."

"Yeah. We saw." Justin says and leans back in his chair.

"So, how did you get away then?" Julia asks. "They destroyed that place."

DJ reaches for the bottle in front of Julia, with a few ounces of whiskey remaining.

Justin grabs the bottle from him.

"Let him have it, Justin." Julia says.

DJ takes the bottle back and takes another small sip, and then hands it back to Justin.

"I was at the creek, a couple of miles away, when it…when it happened. I was refilling our water supply. I drew the short straw that day. I remember cursing the whole time walking down to the creek that day, thinking how unlucky I was. I was on my way back when…when I heard the explosions and gunshots echo through the woods.

And I froze. I just froze. I just cowered and stayed there, hiding in the bushes. I was too scared to move. I stayed there all night. And then, the next day, I built enough courage and made my way back…and I saw what had happened."

Julia leans back and looks down at the floor, thinking about the brothers again.

"And then what? I mean, how did you end up with a news van?" Justin asks quickly.

"Well, I thought that was it for me after that. I mean, I had nowhere else to go. And I didn't trust going back to the last place I was hiding at before there. I felt hopeless. I planned on staying there at their hideout and trying to survive as long as I could with the rations that were still left. But then, that night after they were killed, a news crew showed up to film what had happened. You know how they are, using it as propaganda to scare anyone else like us that was still out there, not infected or against them. But what I saw was an opportunity, and I took it. While they were filming, I hid in one of their vans. After it came back to their news station, I hid again and waited for them all to leave. I broke into their news station that night and hacked into their computer system. I created a reporter profile for myself, as one of them. And that is basically what I have been doing ever since. I stayed in the local area and visited the brother's place frequently, paying my respects. When I created my fake profile, I manipulated it so that I 'worked' alone, and never had to report or answer to anyone. So,

I'm in their system but there is no accountability of me."

"Oh, yeah right! Get the hell out of here!" Justin barks out.

"Shh!" Dave puts a finger on his lips and points to his bedroom.

Justin leans forward, closer to DJ, sitting across from him at the table.

"You expect us to believe that you have been out there, in the plain, wide open? For months? Without getting caught?"

"Justin," Julia says. She looks at him sternly and then at DJ. "How did you hack into their system exactly?"

"It's not that hard, really. I mean, once you…"

"It's not that hard? Are you freaking kidding me?" Justin interrupts him.

"Justin, be quiet." Dave says, staring at him and then back at DJ. "Go ahead, DJ."

DJ looks at Justin for a few seconds and then continues.

"It's not hard to manipulate their data, once you are in their system, on one of their networked computers. And you have to know what you are doing, obviously. They rely too heavily on technology and electronics. Once their network is compromised you can turn all that technology against them. Their greatest strength then becomes their biggest weakness."

"So, you are telling us that you, DJ Paris, a club DJ, hacked into the most powerful group in the world?"

"Well, no. I mean, I hacked into their news network. But, I mean yeah, sort of, I guess. I told you guys I was nerd growing up. Before I went to college, the only friends I had were online. Super…nerd…"

DJ looks at Julia and almost blushes from embarrassment of his own remark, and then he looks away.

Julia leans forward in her chair and stares at him.

"I call BS." Justin spurts out. "We, Robert, has been trying to do that for years. And he has had all kinds of people try to help him, even including people from within AGI. And it took years to bypass the firewalls from within their network. So, I'm not buying it. You're lying. Or…you're a double agent or something."

Justin pulls a gun from his hip and places it on the table toward DJ, holding it firmly.

"Justin. Put the gun away. If he wanted to hurt us or turn us in, he could have done that already. Think about it."

"I am thinking about it, Julia. What if his mission was to find out where our bunker was at before trying to kill us? Did you think about that?"

Julia pauses. She looks at DJ and he looks back at her. She stares at him for a moment and can see the true innocence in his eyes. She believes him.

"Justin, put the gun away."

"Julia, I don't think we should just…"

"Do it. Now, Justin. I believe him."

"Come on, Justin. Put the gun away." Dave says.

Justin looks at Dave and Dave stares back at him with strong, trusting eyes.

"He's just some random guy that helped us. And now, you two believe that insane story he just told us?"

Julia thinks silently for a moment before responding.

"Yeah," Julia says, looking at DJ. "I do."

She looks back at Justin. "And he's not just some random guy, Justin. He helped us, didn't he? And he was driving a news van for crying out loud. How could he make that up? And nobody was after him. And, how would he know so much about the brothers? Think about that, Justin."

Justin stands up quickly, out of frustration.

"Robert is going to have a field day with you after he hears about this croc of…" Justin stops mid-sentence as he stares into Robert's operation room, at the computer monitors. He turns around and looks at DJ, and then moves quickly around the table to his chair. He pulls DJ out of his chair by the shirt collar.

"Justin! Stop it!" Julia raises her voice, trying not to scream and wake up the others.

"Hey, Justin. Come on man." Dave says, as Justin pushes him out of the way.

Justin forces DJ into the operations room and into the chair at the computer desk. He slaps the keyboard on one of the computers.

"Alright, hacker dude. Hack away. Show us what you can do."

"Justin!" Julia says, as her and Dave enter the room.

"No. He said he hacked into The Society's network. So, decrypting one of their files should be a simple walk in the park then. Right? Mr. Black Hat?"

"Black Hat? No, I mean, it was just their news network systems. I never said…"

"Shut up!" Justin places his hand on DJ's hand and puts it on the mouse. "Now, decrypt one of those files."

"Justin, you know Robert doesn't like us messing with those files." Dave says, looking to Julia for support.

She looks back at Dave. Then she looks at Justin, and then stops at DJ. "Do it."

"Julia," Dave pleads.

"I believe him. He can do it."

DJ glances up at Julia. She looks back at him with confidence.

Justin pushes DJ's shoulder. "You heard her, do it."

DJ looks at the computer and takes a deep breath. He moves the cursor on the computer and starts opening folders and then begins typing, and then opening command prompts and functions. He leans closer to the screen and traces his finger along a running line of code.

Justin leans back from the desk and looks a little surprised by what DJ just did in a few seconds.

DJ pulls his hand back from the screen. "Okay, umm…I'm sorry, I…"

"See, I knew it. I told you guys." Justin says.

"No, it's not that, it's…" DJ looks at Julia.

"What? What is it?" She asks.

"Well, this decryption code is kind of…well, it's antiquated. I mean, nobody really uses this type of programming anymore. It's virtually impossible to use these crypto-variables within the coding to decrypt the ciphers and asymmetric algorithm embedded in these files. It would take forever to try and…"

"Wait, hold on. Slow down a minute. What does all that mean? For us non-computer types."

"Okay. Well, umm, what's something that you like? Or used to like? Like a sport or something? I'll try to make an analogy."

"Racing, track car racing." Dave says quickly.

They all turn around and look at him.

"Sorry. I just miss watching it. I even raced a little amateur…never mind. Sorry."

They turn back to DJ.

"Umm…okay. Racing, racing. Okay, so think of it like you are on a racetrack, with all of these other fast racecars. The racecars being the codes. And the racecars all look pretty much the same. And once a race is over, then a new race starts on the same track, with the same cars. Except, you're not racing in a racecar, you are racing in a, umm…well, you are racing in like…"

"Like a regular car," Justin says.

"Umm, no. This code, racecar, that you are in, is more like a bicycle. I mean, yeah, you could eventually finish the race. But, the whole time you are going around the track, these other racecars, being the newer types of code, well they are just flying past you, lapping you even. Which means even when you finish the first race, the other codes have already advanced to other races, and they are hundreds of overall laps ahead of you. And sure, you can still see the other racecars on the track, but you can't tell who's following who, or who's in the lead, because you are so far behind. It just becomes this one, big, confusing race."

Julia and Justin look at each other and somewhat understand the analogy.

"So, you can't open them?"

"No, I can. But not without modifying and upgrading the decryption keys and algorithms. You know, changing from a bicycle to an actual racecar. I'm actually surprised your dad was able to open the couple of files that he did. I mean, it must have taken weeks, maybe even months, to get them open with using this old style of coding."

Julia sees the doubt fading from Justin's face because DJ is spot on with his assessment.

"How long will it take to open a file?" Justin asks. "After you change the code, how long will it take?"

"Well, that all depends on the level of encryption on the file itself. Hang on."

DJ browses through some of the files and their properties. "This one is pretty simple here. I could probably open it in fifteen minutes, maybe even less."

"Do it," Julia says. "Change the coding."

"Hey, guys, let's think about this for a second." Dave says calmly. "Julia, are you sure you want to do this? I mean, what if it erases what Robert has done so far?"

Julia looks at him with certainty, and Dave sees that there is no talking her out of it.

"Do it," Julia says to DJ again.

DJ smiles at her confidence in him.

Julia sees that Justin notices their brief eye contact and she quickly focuses back to the computer screen.

Justin shakes his head.

They all watch patiently and anxiously for the next few minutes as DJ plucks away at the keyboard. He then punches a few more keys, slowing down, and then he leans back and lets out a small sigh.

"Okay," DJ says, turning around in the chair to face them. "It's hard to say exactly how fast the file will open. I picked the smallest one, one just to show you that I know what I'm talking about, and that I'm not…"

"No way," Justin cuts him off.

They all lean towards the screen, observing the new plain text file that just opened.

DJ spins back around. Julia looks at him and smiles.

They were all impressed. They were all relieved. And, they were all hopeful.

"That is, uh…well, I definitely believe you now. I mean, you are definitely, positively, a complete and total, super nerd." Justin says.

"Thanks. I think." DJ replies.

"No, this is great. I mean it. Really great." Justin says, while giving him a smile of acceptance.

"Yeah, it's…amazing." Dave concurs.

Julia looks at DJ and just smiles at him, along with Justin and Dave.

DJ smiles back at them, modestly.

Justin backs up from the group and looks at Dave and Julia, "We need to call Robert."

Julia thinks about it for a moment before responding. "I think we have done enough for one day. Let's get a little rest and call him in the morning."

"Okay, but first thing in the morning. We have to tell him about this." Justin concedes to Julia's request.

"Goodnight," Justin and Dave both say to Julia and DJ, as they leave the operations room.

"Well, I guess I'll show you where you can sleep." Julia puts on her headlamp and hands DJ one from the computer desk, "Follow me."

Julia walks down the narrow hallway and past Brian's room. She pauses and shines her light in his room for a brief second. She sees him sleeping quietly and then she continues walking further down the hallway. She slides a door open, past the generator room, and enters a larger, open bay room, with several mattresses and over a dozen cots on the floor. She makes her way to the far corner and turns on a floor lamp.

The room lightens up from the battery powered light and she takes her headlamp off.

DJ looks around the room.

"It's not exactly a five-star hotel, but…"

"No, it's fine." DJ quickly cuts her off. "Really, it's fine. Trust me, I am used to staying in worse places than this. I mean, this whole bunker, it's amazing. You guys built all this?"

"My dad," Julia says, taking a small breath and looking down.

"Where exactly is he right now?"

"Out East. He is trying to find the other contacts we had helping us. That's what we were doing too. We went one way and he went another, to cover more ground faster."

"Well, I can't wait to meet him. I mean, what he did, what you all did…it really gave us hope out there."

Julia smiles at the comment and then pulls some blankets out of a storage container and hands them to DJ. They look at each other in the eyes for a few seconds, as their hands gently meet under the blankets.

Julia pulls her hands away, "Yeah, well, I'll see you in the morning then."

DJ nods and she turns on her headlamp.

She stops at the doorway just before she exits.

"Umm, there is a toilet behind that curtain over there, and there is some bottled water in that storage closet there." Julia says and points.

"Thanks," DJ replies, looking around for a second and then back at her.

Julia raises her shirt, just enough to expose the small handgun on her hip.

"Even though I trust you, don't go wondering around the bunker on your first night."

"Absolutely not. You got it." DJ responds quickly.

Julia smiles and leaves the room.

DJ lets out a small sigh and looks around the room. He sits down on a mattress beside the lamp. He takes off his boots and turns off the lamp, and the room fills with complete darkness. A few seconds go by and he turns the lamp back on. "Yep, definitely leaving that on."

* * *

DJ wakes up to the light and pleasant hum of a generator running from the other room across from him. He can see the hallway outside the room, filled with a mild, amber light.

He sits up on the mattress and begins putting his boots on, and then hears a light conversation from the kitchen as he exits the room and into the hallway.

DJ stops at the first room on the right as he passes it, noticing a boy sitting at a small table in the room by himself.

Brian looks up at DJ in the doorway.

"Hi, I'm DJ. I just got here last night."

Brian looks at him for a moment without saying anything, and then continues playing the board game by himself.

"DJ, hey. Come join us in the kitchen for breakfast."

DJ looks at Justin standing in the kitchen, and then he looks back at the boy again, "Yeah, coming."

DJ enters the kitchen and sees that everyone is there.

Amy puts Samantha down on the floor and stands up. Samantha picks up a small toy from the floor and runs off into the bedroom.

DJ smiles as the child brushes his leg as she quickly runs past him.

"Have a seat," Amy says.

"Thanks."

Amy sets a bowl of oatmeal down in front of him and pours some hot water in it, stirring it lightly with a spoon for him.

"I'm Amy, Dave's wife. And that was our daughter, Samantha."

"Nice to meet you. I'm DJ Pa…DJ, just call me DJ."

Amy smiles at his innocent nature and tone, already knowing the full story on his name from Dave.

"Nice to meet you too, DJ."

She takes a small plate with canned meat away from Dave and places in front of DJ.

Dave tries to grab a piece of meat from the plate before she lets go of it, and Amy gives him a quick glare. Dave pulls his hand back.

"There is plenty to go around, DJ. Help yourself."

"Thank you, ma'am."

"Amy, call me Amy. I'm not that old yet." She says, smiling.

There's a moment of silence around the table, and then everyone continues eating quietly.

Amy leaves and goes into the bedroom with Samantha.

Julia finishes eating and stands up from the table, and then grabs a metal box from the floor. Justin gets up after her and picks up his rifle and backpack from the corner of the kitchen.

"DJ, stay here with Dave and keep working on the files. Me and Justin are going to go outside and try to get ahold of Robert."

DJ nods with a mouthful of food.

Justin and Julia leave the kitchen and head into the bunker tunnel, toward the hatch opening access.

Dave looks over to DJ and smiles, "Well kid, I guess we can start getting to know each other a little better, since you're one of us now."

TWENTY-TWO

Three days go by.

DJ continues decrypting files every day and adjusts to bunker life. He gets to know everyone, and everyone gets to know him a little better. And everyone welcomes him as a new member, as one of them.

Dave, Amy, and their daughter, all enjoy the new spark of life and change in the bunker.

Julia tends to Brian as normal and he shows no change to her coming back.

Julia and Justin take turns calling Robert every day, but every day they are unsuccessful in reaching him. All his phones are turned off and go straight to a 'no longer in service' message. Robert was supposed to be back already. Justin and Julia arrived a few days earlier than scheduled, but now was the time when they all should have returned.

By the end of the third day, and still no contact with Robert, everyone in the bunker begins to worry, and tension starts to overshadow the brief phase of hope and excitement that DJ had brought with him.

Even though it was against their protocol, and Robert's specific guidance, Justin and Julia plan on going back out the following morning. They were going to find Robert.

* * *

"So, you're really leaving tomorrow morning, huh?" DJ asks at the corner of Julia's room.

Julia puts down a book she has read over a dozen times before and looks up from her bed at DJ.

"Yeah. He's my dad. I have to."

"Yeah, absolutely. Well, I just wanted to say, be safe out there. I plan on working on a few more files tonight. Some of them that have video and audio are taking a little longer to open, but I'm getting there. Well, I'll let you get some rest."

"It's great, what you are doing. Thank you for working on that stuff. Robert is probably going to have a heart attack when he sees how many files you have already opened in just a few days."

"Well, if I fall asleep before you leave in the morning, I just wanted to tell you good luck. And be safe."

Julia smiles softly at him.

"Goodnight, Julia."

"Night." Julia keeps smiling to herself and turns off her lamp.

DJ gets to work on the computers again.

After a few hours and finally opening another audio file, he takes a break and heads to the kitchen to eat something. All lamps were off in the bunker, except the kitchen and operations room. He is the only one awake.

DJ finishes a can of processed meat and vegetables. He gets up from the table and pours another cup of coffee, cold, and somewhat stale from being brewed hours before. He pours a cap of whiskey into the coffee, leaving one small shot still left in the bottle. He takes a small whiff and stirs the coffee and whiskey combo with his finger.

Something catches the corner of his eye as he takes a drink. A subtle flash of light from the operations room. He looks around the kitchen and the other dark, surrounding rooms, verifying that the light did not come from anywhere else. He shakes his head and takes another small drink. The light blinks again as his back is turned to the operations room. He turns around and there was nothing.

He walks back into the operations room and looks around the room carefully. He stares at the small, red beacon light, in the back-corner ceiling of the room. He takes a seat behind the computer and drinks his coffee, watching the light.

Five minutes go by. Nothing. He shakes it off as being nothing more than his eyes playing tricks on him, or a glitch in the light.

"Okay, let's get to know each other. File nine, one, two, seven, six, five, zero, zero, three.

Also known as, BL twenty-twenty." He says to himself out loud, staring at the file.

He places his earphones in and presses play on an outdated MP3 player. He begins typing a new algorithm and code into the computer to decrypt the file.

After more than another hour of working on the computer, DJ feels a light breeze of air come from behind him. His heartbeat instantly speeds up as he senses someone is there, and then he feels a cold, hard piece of metal at the base of his neck. The music continues playing as he sits there frozen, knowing he now had a gun to his head, and that it is probably Robert holding it.

Not wanting to get shot, he tries to control his breathing and plead his case over the music blaring in his ears.

"I can't hear you, Mr. Rawlings. My earphones. Can you please take them out? Then I can explain who I am."

He feels the earphones slide slowly out of his left ear, then his right.

"Don't make any sudden movements. Now, who are you? And what are you doing here?"

"I'm DJ Paris. Frank, I mean, Francis Alvarez, that's my real name. Justin and Julia brought me back here. I helped them, please, just ask one of…"

"Shut up. You are not a contact. So, why did they bring you here?" Robert asks, digging the gun further into his neck.

"Robert, Mr. Rawlings, please. Just ask them, sir. They will tell you…"

"Dad?" Julia asks from behind them, standing in the kitchen.

"Dad! We thought something happened to you." Julia says, walking quickly into the room and seeing the situation.

She looks at Robert and places her hand on the gun, slowly lowering it away from DJ's head. "He's okay Dad, he helped us, he is helping us. He's okay, really. I promise."

Robert places the weapon on safe and holsters it on his side.

DJ lets out a deep sigh of relief as he turns around slowly.

Robert hugs Julia.

"It's good to see you. Is everyone here okay? Is Justin…"

"Yeah, yeah. We're all fine, Dad. We were actually going out to look for you in the morning. So…thanks, I guess. For saving us the trip." Julia smiles and they let each other go.

Robert stares back at DJ.

"Well, Dad, this is DJ. DJ, this is my Dad, Robert Rawlings."

DJ stands up slowly to shake his hand.

"Yeah, we've met already." Robert says, still untrustingly, and still uncomfortable with someone he does not know being in the bunker with them.

DJ pulls his empty hand back, without a handshake.

"Umm, sir, I think the warning light might need replaced or something. They said it should go off if someone enters an access point, but I think it only flashed like once or twice. And well, you definitely caught me off guard, sir."

Robert lets out a sigh and pulls up the camera footage on an extended monitor display.

"That is why the camera footage always stays up on one of these computer monitors here. And there is nothing wrong with the lights, kid. I designed this place. I think I know how to disarm one of the sensors if I want to."

Julia silently apologizes to DJ with her eyes. DJ looks at her, and Robert looks at the two of them. DJ looks away quickly and down at the floor.

"And Julia, what are you thinking? Why in the world did you let him touch my computers in the first place?"

"Well, I told you he has been helping us. He knows a lot about computers. So, he has been unlocking and decrypting files over the past couple of days. And he's opened way more than just a few of them."

Robert looks at her and DJ, with frustration and anger still on his face.

"Move."

DJ moves quickly away from the computer and stands beside Julia.

Robert leans over the desk and minimizes the two screens with program code running across them. He expands the main folder with the encrypted files.

"I have been working on these files for months. I swear, if you slowed down my progress in even the slightest little…"

Robert goes mute and looks in harder at the screen, not believing what he is looking at. He looks back at them quickly, and then back at the screen. He lets out a long, deep and cheerful sigh. A sigh that is full of relief, and accomplishment, as if he had just won a championship game and he is completely exhausted from playing in it.

Julia looks over at DJ and smiles. For a few brief seconds, she gently grips his left, ring and pinky fingers, with her right, index and middle fingers. DJ smiles back and looks away, blushing slightly. She lets go as soon as Robert starts turning around, towards them.

"You have opened over thirty files here. I'm…well…I'm at a loss for words really."

Robert smiles and takes a seat, sitting quietly for a moment. "Thank you. Thank you."

"Sir, can I ask you a question?"

"Yeah, sure. I would like to ask you some questions too," Robert laughs out.

"Well, it's just that, I read most of the files I opened, but some of them didn't really make any sense to me. What does it all mean?"

"Well, I need to go over all of the, thirty something new files that you opened. But, the answers to everything we need know about The Society and how the TSOMBIE program works, is all right here in these files. The last chance of how to get our freedom back, everyone's freedom, is all right here."

Robert smiles at DJ and Julia.

"Oh man. I mean, this, is, amazing. It really is. I can't believe it." Robert smiles at the computer screen for a few more moments.

Robert lets out a small yawn that surprises even himself, and he looks down at his watch.

"Well, now that we are clearly way ahead of schedule, I would like to get a long and peaceful, full night of sleep. And, we are all back now, so we can all relax a little bit. I'm sure I had you guys worried with my phones off. We can start going over all of this stuff tomorrow, when I am fresh."

Robert stands and hugs Julia. He turns, and with his left arm still wrapped around Julia, he extends his right hand to DJ.

DJ smiles and shakes his hand.

"Welcome to the team, DJ."

TWENTY-THREE

"Here you go, sweetie. Mike?"

Melissa places her hand on Mike's shoulder, startling him. "Hello in there?"

"Sorry. Thanks, honey."

Mike takes the cup of coffee from his wife and places it down on his desk, in one of the few empty spaces that remain amongst a sloppy collage of files and photos. He smiles briefly at his wife and then continues reading the stack of papers in front of him.

"Right. Okay. I guess I will bring you lunch in a little while then. What do you want?"

"Yeah. Thanks." Mike says, as he continues reading.

"And, I am going to burn all of our clothes and drive our cars into the pool. Is that okay?"

"Okay. Thanks, honey."

"Mike! Mike! Stop and look at me."

He stops reading and looks up at her, surprised. "What? What's wrong?"

"What's wrong? Mike, you are completely spaced out in here. You have not left this room in days. I have only seen you sleep maybe a few hours each night. You have not showered. I mean, don't you think this is a little too much? That you might be overdoing it just a little bit? I mean, is finding him worth putting yourself through all of this? Putting us through all of this? I would rather you just stay at work if this is all you are going to do when you are here at home. Because you are not really here anymore, not your mind anyways."

They look at each other for a moment, and then yelling and the sound of their young boys running through the house breaks up the silence.

She closes her eyes and tilts her head toward the ceiling. "Boys! Stop running in the house!"

She turns to leave, and Mike grabs her hand. "Melissa. Hey, I'm sorry. I'm sorry."

She turns around and looks at him with watery eyes.

"You're right. I have been overdoing it. I promise that I am going to take a break today and spend time with you guys. I promise. You and the boys are more important to me than work, I swear. But if I do not find Rawlings, then I would not be providing the best future for you and the kids. I'm not trying to find him for my father, or for The Society. I am going to find him for…"

"Mom! Jack hit me!" The youngest son yells from somewhere in the house.

She closes her eyes again and Mike pulls her into him at the chair, and he hugs her waist tightly. She smiles and leans down, kissing his forehead.

"Alright boys, here I come! Stop playing and clean your rooms! I mean it this time!" She says loudly, but still in a happier tone than before.

Mike smiles as her voice fades after exiting his study. He looks at the mess of files and pictures and maps on his desk. He lets out a sigh and starts shuffling them around, attempting to put them back into some type of logical order.

After a few minutes, Jack bursts through his door and runs up to him.

"Hey. Your mom just said no more running. Right?" Mike puts his arm around his son, still holding some papers in his hand.

Zack enters the room and darts toward them. Jack runs around the other side of Mike's desk, and then the two boys start yelling at each other and then at their father.

"Dad, Zack's trying to hit me!"

"He hit me first!"

"Hey! Boys! Take it outside. And no more hitting each other. Got it?"

The brothers smile devilishly at each other, holding on to opposite sides of Mike's desk. Jack pushes off the desktop and runs out the balcony doors of the office, outside and onto the lawn. Zack gives pursuit, bumping the edge of the desk and sending a whirlwind of files and photos to the floor.

"Zack! Zack! Get back here and clean this up!" Mike stands and watches as the boys run wild outside in the large backyard. Mike smiles and lets out a deep sigh, shaking his head at the new clutter on the floor.

He bends down and starts putting the photos back in a binder. He pauses. He pulls one of the photos closer to his face.

It was an older picture of Julia Rawlings, when she was just a kid.

Mike recognizes the image and remembers studying it before, at least a dozen times. But he didn't remember noticing the small reflection in the truck mirror that Julia was leaning on in the picture.

There is a small outline of a brown sign in the sideview mirror, like a state park sign. 'een The Lak' are the only letters visible in the small reflection.

Mike closes his eyes and tries to think of what the name on the sign could be.

A few minutes go by and his eyes flash open, wide and confident. He knows the name.

Mike jams the photo in his pocket and quickly grabs a few select files, and then begins rushing to leave his house.

"Mike? Mike? Hang on. Where are you going?"

Mike lets go of the front doorknob and walks to the bottom of the staircase, waiting for his wife to finish walking down to him.

"I found something. I think. But I need to run to the office for a little while and check it out. I'll call you. Okay?"

"Dressed like that? And without even taking a..."

Mike leans forward and kisses her on the lips in mid-sentence. And then he runs out of the house, leaving the front door wide-open.

*　*　*

"Scott," Mike mumbles, out of breath as he barges into Scott's office.

Scott looks out to Mike from a wall-closet in the back of the office. "Mike. Hey, I was just about to grab some lunch at the club. Care to join me?"

Scott pulls a coat out and closes the closet door. He looks back at Mike, bending over and breathing hard.

"Mike? You okay? And what are you wearing? You just come from the gym or something?"

Mike stands upright and walks slowly over to Scott's desk.

"Scott...I found something. But...I need control of the...camera system network...to confirm it." Mike gasps out slowly.

"Okay. Well, why don't you just tell me what it is, and I'll look into it. You look like you could still use a little more time off anyways. And smell like it too."

Mike slams his hands on the desk. "No!" He takes a deep, controlled breath. "Please, Scott."

"Okay, Mike. You can use the camera network."

"And...I need the access code for satellite control."

"Come on now, Mike. You know I can't approve that. Satellite requests need to get approved through Tasha."

"I can't go through all of the red-tape bureaucracy on this one, Scott. Please."

Mike looks at Scott for his approval, but Scott looks down and away.

"You owe me, Scott."

Scott snaps his head up quickly, "What makes you think that I owe you anything, Mike?"

They stare at each other and Mike looks slowly around the office, methodically. The office that used to be his.

"No. Okay, no. I didn't steal your job, Mike. They put me in here. You know that."

Mike puts his hands on the large executive desk and looks up at Scott, sincerely now.

"A few hours, Scott. That's all I am asking for here."

Scott lets out a small sigh of frustration and puts on his coat. He walks around the edge of the desk and pauses, standing closely beside Mike.

Mike closes his eyes and bows his head toward the desk.

"I didn't tell you this," Scott whispers. "We never had this conversation. You understand?"

Mike opens his eyes and looks up at him.

"Keep looking forward," Scott says quietly. "Alpha...one...one...three. You have two hours,

Mike. I'll give you two hours. If you don't find anything by then, I will have to report it as unauthorized access."

Mike looks at him and nods with gratitude.

Scott stops at the door on the way out. "Good luck, Mike. I mean that."

Mike watches Scott clear everyone from the crowded department floor.

"Let's go people! Department luncheon at the club, everybody out!" Scott repeats himself around the room as he exits.

Scott's assistant, Chris, catches up to him in the hallway.

"Sir, what did Mike want?"

"Nothing important. Same old stuff, just Mike being Mike."

Mike waits for the last few TSOMBIE analysts to leave and then he walks over to the main control panel desk in the middle of the now-empty department. He logs into the system and begins pulling up camera footage files over the past couple of years, along with aerial maps, all in close vicinity of the campgrounds and park area from the picture.

He studies over the footage and begins writing down traffic patterns of certain vehicles and their descriptions, and taking still shot frames of their license plates.

After he takes several notes, he begins the process of elimination, still not exactly sure what vehicle or vehicles he is looking for. But, he remains confident that something would reveal itself.

A little over an hour goes by.

Mike wipes his eyes, fatigued from the intense search effort. He still had not found anything significant. He looks at his watch and a sense of urgency starts creeping in.

He decides to change the search parameters, expanding the radius and observing more aerial footage from satellites, instead of from the ground-level cameras.

Another thirty minutes go by. Nothing.

Mike looks at his watch again. He comes up with another idea. He starts reviewing footage from the present and working his way backwards, instead of starting in the past.

He looks at his watch again, and then at the department doors. He speeds up the rewind of the footage.

"Come on, come on," he says quietly at the monitor.

A few minutes go by and he pauses the satellite footage. A vehicle in the middle of nowhere. He runs the video forward a little, and then backwards again, covering the span of about five miles in an isolated area of the forest imagery. He plays the looped footage again and then pauses it again. He looks at the date. It was just from the day before.

A vehicle seemed to simply disappear into the woods on the video. The only structure remotely close to the vehicle was a small, isolated cabin, miles away from where the vehicle seemed to vanish. There was no official listing for an address of the cabin. And it was not property of the state park.

Mike pulls up camera footage from the ground around the same general area, and during the same date range. The closest camera was several miles away, near a small gas station.

After a few minutes, he freezes the frame and writes down the license plate. He pulls up the aerial and ground footage still-frames and compares them.

It was the same car. Late-model, black, luxury sedan.

He runs the license plate number into another computer program and looks back at the department doors.

"Come on," he says quietly again.

A registered name and address pops up. He quickly types the address into the GPS program and it shows up, almost thirty miles away. It is registered to a regular TSOMBIE civilian. He pulls up the record on the civilian and opens the phone tracking program.

The civilian had never broken routine over the past two years. And the man's phone had never been in that area where the car disappeared into the woods, and that car had never been parked at the civilian's house, or even driven past it for that matter.

Mike knows he is close now and that he is finally onto something. His hands begin to shake with nervousness and excitement.

He runs the plate and vehicle description through another database program. Several hits start popping up for the black sedan, but they all have different license plate numbers. It is after all, a somewhat common car, Mike thinks to himself. He starts eliminating hits from other states around the country, too far away to be the same one within the date range.

Then, he notices a familiar pattern starting to appear as he deletes the unprobeable hits. Three of the hits were all in close vicinity of raids that had been conducted on the individuals that were involved with the bombings. All contacts of Rawlings. He pulls up the ground footage from the three raid locations in different Eastern states. The first two did not provide anything useful, other than the car itself.

Then, Mike completely stops moving after he opens the last image, a head shot photo that was captured through the vehicle's front windshield, from a highway camera. The facial recognition of Robert Rawlings was as clear as daylight to Mike, even under the mild camouflage of an obvious wig and dyed facial hair.

All of Mike's emotions begin rushing through his body at one time. All the heartache. All the stress. All the past failures. And all the countless attempts, and unrewarding effort that was spent on finding this one man.

He laughs to himself and plops down in the chair.

"I did it," he says softly. He chuckles a few more times and yells, "I did it!"

"Did what?" Chris asks, sneaking up on him. Chris shakes his head at all the images on the screens, and at the computers and satellite programs running.

"You did it alright. You've gone too far, Mike. Ms. McNeil is going to lose her mind when she hears about you accessing these systems."

Mike laughs a little. He wipes his face and then stands up.

"I think I am going to tell her myself. Right now, as a matter of fact. But, accessing the systems won't be what she really loses her mind about."

Before Chris could respond, Mike takes off running out of the department and shouts, "I am back!"

Chris watches him leave, somewhat confused by his ranting. He turns back to the main control center and shakes his head again, looking at everything Mike had accessed. He notices an image of a man in a vehicle. He looks closer and projects the image onto the large wall-screen.

He just stares at the screen, motionless for a moment, in utter disbelief.

"Holy…you have got to be kidding me."

* * *

Michael Hardy looks at his vibrating phone during a small, Inner Circle meeting, in the new Society headquarters building. 'Mike Calling' blinks on the phone screen. He turns the phone to silent and places it face-up on the table.

He continues listening to the briefer in the meeting as the phone continues to light up for several minutes, and then finally stops.

The meeting concludes after another ten minutes, and Mr. Hardy tries calling Mike back. It goes straight to voicemail. He then calls Tasha.

"...Hello Tasha, I need you to do me a favor. Get ahold of Mike and find out what he needs. He kept calling me during my meeting and now he won't answer. Keep sending me your updates on his activity and keep a close eye on him. I feel like he might go off the rails after his unsuccessful trip to the bloodline camp. I want to keep a tight lid on him until after the elections, just like we talked about."

Before Tasha could finish responding on the other end of the phone call, Mike bursts into her office.

"…Understood, sir. I'll get right on that." Tasha hangs up and looks at Mike, storming towards her desk.

"Hi there, Mike. You know, that is so strange, because I was just thinking…"

"I found him!" He says, aggressively interrupting Tasha's normal, sarcastic voice.

"You, found him? Found who? Raw…"

"Yes, Rawlings. I, me…I found him. I, did it."

Mike can see the slight shade of panic in her face, knowing that this news would put him right back at the front of the line again.

Mike masks his happiness fairly well, but Tasha struggles to conceal her anger and anxiety. She reaches for a cigarette.

"Wow, that's uh…how? How did you find him? Where is he?"

Mike relaxes even more after hearing the faint crackling in her voice, and he takes a seat. He sits quietly for a moment and enjoys the slight satisfaction of making her wait eagerly for the information.

"I tracked a vehicle that showed up to three raid locations in different Eastern states, several weeks after the raids had occurred. And I tracked that same vehicle to an isolated cabin, in Tennessee. Well, close to the border of Tennessee and Kentucky."

"And umm, how exactly did you confirm this?"

Mike knows where she is going with the question. He thinks about his answer but then realizes it doesn't matter. He found Rawlings. And neither his father, nor anyone else in The Society, would care if he broke some of the rules in the process.

"I accessed the camera system network, and the satellites." Mike responds with calm confidence.

Tasha sits quietly and knows that she can't do anything to Mike for what he did.

"Now, I need to tell him. Where is he at today? I tried calling him earlier, but he didn't answer."

"Look, Mike. Why don't you just show me exactly what you have? Let me confirm this. And then, we can both tell your father, together."

Mike looks at Tasha's phone and sees a text message flashing, his father's name is at the top of the screen. He grabs her phone.

"Mike, wait a minute…"

Before she could talk him down, Mike had already dialed.

"No, it's Mike…Yes, sir, I am standing in her office right now…Well, I wanted to tell you in person, but I did it. I finally found Rawlings…Yes, sir…I am, sir, one hundred percent, sir…I'm positive about it, one hundred percent…I will be sure to tell her…Yes, sir…Thank you, Dad…I will."

Mike hangs up.

Tasha puffs away at the small cigarette and lights another, her blood pressure slightly boiling and changing the pigmentation in her cheeks.

Mike gently places her phone down and slides it slowly across her desk with his hand.

"He would like for you to call him, to discuss the details of the operation to capture Rawlings. And I..."

Scott enters the office and interrupts. "Mike? I've been looking for you. Chris told me."

Scott conceals his smile and holds silent his congratulatory remarks in front of Tasha.

"Tasha, look, I can explain."

"Did you know about this?" Tasha asks quickly. "Did you know what he was doing, Scott?"

Scott looks at Mike, and he didn't want to lie to Tasha. Mike's courage and achievement was too inspiring for him to back down to her, even though telling her would be career suicide for him.

"Yes. I knew. And I gave him the access codes."

Mike respectfully nods to Scott.

Tasha exhales and cringes at the two of them.

"Thank you. Thank you for being honest, Scott. You're fired. Mike, congratulations. Your old job just opened back up."

"What? No, I..."

Scott puts his hand out, "It's okay, Mike. It's fine." Scott remains calm, not wanting to become an outright enemy of Tasha.

"Okay then, analyst, you can leave my office and get back to work."

Mike watches Scott leave the office and feels sympathy for him, but then he quickly turns his focus back to Tasha.

"I want in on this operation, Tasha."

"Of course, Mike. Of course. I have to come down and get your analysis and…"

"No, I mean 'in' the operation itself. I want to be on the ground, with the capture teams."

"Mike, we don't really want to…"

"It's not a negotiation, Tasha. Look, I don't care about this job. And I don't care about you and me fighting about who is going to take over one day. You can have it. But, I am going to be the one that looks him in the eyes when he is caught. I am going to be the one that brings him in. I am going to be there."

Tasha is thrown off a little by his remarks about stepping aside from future leadership. She exhales and thinks for a minute about what he said.

"Yes, you're right, Mike. You found him. It should be you that brings him in. You will be embedded with the entry team on the ground tonight."

Mike is somewhat surprised by her quick acceptance, and then realizes what he just said to her, that she could have his position at the top. He doesn't care though, because he knows The Society will override the decision and put him back at the top, regardless of their little verbal agreement.

Tasha breaks the moment of silence and stands up. "Now, let's go down and look over your findings, so I can start planning this mission, for us."

TWENTY-FOUR

Everyone in the bunker sits speechless on the sofa in Robert's operation room.

They were all overwhelmed by the updated brief that Robert and DJ had just given, compiled from all the files DJ had opened over the past few days. Robert had recovered the walls of the entire room with new notes, new and more highlighted areas on the maps, and there were new names and locations of all immune, non-Society bloodlines. The intimacy and amount of details from the decrypted files about The Society and TSOMBIE program was simply, overwhelming.

"And now, I have saved the best for the last. DJ, hit it." Robert and DJ smile at their corny attempt at a joke.

The others just shake their heads, somewhat exhausted from the detailed brief.

Robert cups his hand to his ear and closes his eyes.

"You guys hear that? Do you hear that? We did it! We finally did it! We found out the primary method of how they send messages to TSOMBIEs, how they control people. This is the main reason I wanted to give you guys an updated brief today."

"Wait, hear what Dad?" Julia asks.

"Yeah, I don't hear anything either." Justin says.

Robert looks to Dave and Amy. They shake their heads, no.

"DJ, turn it up." Robert smiles again, and DJ turns up the volume on the speakers.

Robert opens his eyes wider and looks around at each of them. They all shake their heads again, no.

"I mean, I hear a really faint hum coming through the speaker. It just sounds like the power buzz or something though." Dave says, as little Samantha squirms out of his lap.

Robert points at Dave and jumps a little, "That's it! That, is, it, Davey boy!" He almost sings out.

They all laugh and smile at Robert's uncharacteristic display of excitement. Samantha mimics Robert's body movements and repeats, "dat's it, dat's it."

Robert passes a sheet of paper to the group, with several formulas written on it.

"It's called binaural beat perception. It's basically an auditory illusion, created by multiple harmonic wave tones, with small dichotic differences between two or more frequencies."

DJ nods in agreeance from behind the computer.

"No wonder you two hit it off so good." Julia says, referencing their similar intelligence for being a reason Robert had so quickly taken to someone that he knew for just a few days.

It was definitely out of the norm for Robert, but it made Julia happy to see her father so happy. His mood really affected everyone else's. So, his new-found joy was welcomed, by all of them.

"Umm, what about..."

"What about people with hearing problems?" DJ cuts Justin off.

"Yeah. What about that?"

Robert hands out another sheet of paper, with several barcode images and several trademarked logos of popular companies and brands.

"We also decoded their files on visual messaging techniques. There are several subliminal messages embedded in those images right there. And they basically create sensory pathways to the cerebral cortex. Same as the audio. Which allows reception of the messages by TSOMBIEs. And well, you already know what they do, or have done, to people with disabilities that are not suited for

Phase Three injections, the ones not selected to be TSOMBIEs."

Robert's tone changes just a little.

"This is amazing. It's amazing, Dad." Julia says, shifting focus back to the positive.

"Yeah. It is, isn't it? I still almost can't believe it. I mean, with this information, we really stand a chance now. We can really do something. But, before we start planning anything, we need to really celebrate this breakthrough. Justin, grab the bottle for us."

Justin looks at Julia and Dave before he answers. "We umm…well, we finished the ration already, Robert. Sorry."

Robert nods quickly. "Okay, no problem, no problem." He looks at his watch. "I'll go for a resupply run."

"Dad, no. I'll go." Julia says. "You've been working so hard in here on all this, and we finished it, so…"

"No, I'll go. I am completely full of energy right now. It will be good for me to walk and get some of it out."

"I'll go with you then," Dave says.

"How about this? You guys all stay here, relax, and cook a nice, big dinner. With the special meat. Huh? And when I get back, we can have a real party. And do it up right. Sound good?"

They all concede and smile at the sound of his idea.

Robert immediately begins prepping for the resupply walk to the cabin.

Everyone leaves the operations room and Julia stops at the doorway. She watches Robert get ready.

He puts on his backpack and they lock eyes for a moment. Robert smiles as he walks over to her.

"I'm so proud of you, Julia."

"I'm proud of you, Dad." She says back, and then hugs him for a moment.

Robert kisses her gently on her forehead. "Alright, I'll be back soon."

Julia watches quietly as he disappears into the hallway, towards the tunnel entrance. Smiling. Full of love. Full of happiness.

*   *   *

Scott sits at his new analyst workstation. He watches Mike suit up with tactical gear through the glass windows of the director's office. He sees Chris leave the office and start walking towards him. Scott turns his chair back to his computer screen.

"Mike, I mean Mr. Hardy, wants to talk with you."

Scott turns to Chris and nods.

Chris watches as Scott walks to the office.

Scott knocks on the open door.

"Come in, Scott."

Scott enters and waits quietly in front of his old desk.

Mike looks at his watch and then finishes strapping on his thigh holster. He holsters his gun and looks at Scott.

"I want you to take over for Chris. I want you to be my right-hand."

Scott looks out of the window at Chris, walking around the main control station.

"Are you sure? I know Chris has been…"

"I don't trust him anymore. I don't trust a lot of people anymore for that matter. But, I trust you, Scott."

"Okay, sure. If that's what you want me to do, then I'll do it. I don't think Tasha is going to like it too much though."

"Let me worry about her." Mike smiles at him. Then he looks at his watch again. "Alright, I need to get on this flight before it takes off. I'll do a communication check with you after I get in the air."

Scott nods and watches him leave the office, ready for the mission.

"Good luck, Mike."

Mike waves and then starts a light jog out of the department.

Scott walks to the main control station and looks at the kaleidoscope of different maps and satellite feeds on the large wall of screens in the front of the department.

Chris hands him the headset and moves to the side, slowly taking a seat and looking forward, appearing to be somewhat depressed and embarrassed.

Scott puts on the headset and flips the broadcast switch on.

He covers the headset microphone, "Chris, bring up satellites two, five, and eight." He uncovers the mic. "Alright people, we are a go for final checks at all stations and mission personnel. Respond in sequence when complete."

Scott looks around at all the TSOMBIE analysts at their workstations, robotically focused on their tasks. Scott's sense of anxiousness and excitement at the importance of this mission fades as he looks at them, knowing that they did not feel it. They didn't feel anything anymore.

* * *

Tasha watches from her office window at the formation of helicopters, fading away into the skyline.

She presses '1' on her office phone.

"Birds are in the air, sir. I think now would be a good time to confirm your approval for Plan B. To completely eliminate the chance of an escape."

Tasha grins wickedly to herself and waits for a response.

*　*　*

Mike struggles to keep pace with the TSOMBIE agents through the woods. The night vision devices are affecting his ability to move as quickly as them.

He slows the team down again over the radio and looks around at them in the dark when he catches up. Several greenish men begin appearing in his goggles, all with weapons and taking a knee in the forest.

Mike gives the signal to move forward again. A few minutes later and the lead agent halts the formation, and then they all encircle on Mike.

Mike adjusts the focus on his goggles and sees the outline of the cabin from the edge of the woods.

"Confirm heat signature," Mike whispers to an agent with a different style of googles on.

The agent gives a 'thumbs up' to Mike.

Mike takes a minute and lets out a few deep breaths.

"Okay. Let's go get him," Mike says. He steps off fast toward the cabin and immediately falls to the ground, panting moderately and reaching for the lower half of his left leg that was now lodged in a deep hole in the ground.

"Hold. Stop." Mike grunts in pain, pulling his leg back out of the hole. "Get the team medic up here."

Mike lies back on the ground and breathes hard.

An agent arrives from the back of the formation and assesses Mike's injury.

"Sir, you have torn some ligaments in your knee, and your ankle is possibly fractured. You are not capable of walking on it right now, sir."

Mike shakes his head and looks at his leg. He shifts his weight and tries to sit up. He lets out a sigh, knowing he could not stand.

The medic was right.

"Okay. Okay. Give me a minute to think."

Mike curses to himself for getting this close and then getting hurt from something so silly like falling in a hole. He lets out a few more deep breaths.

"Okay. Entry Team Leader. I want you to take over and continue mission. I'll maintain overall mission control from here, at the wood line."

Mike leans his back against a tree and the medic begins triaging his injuries on sight, with wraps and injections of numbing anesthetic.

Mike puts his goggles back on. He continues grunting in pain as he watches the team move across the small opening in the forest, toward the cabin.

A couple of minutes later, several flashlights begin dancing around, inside of the dark cabin.

"Target secure," is repeated twice over the radio by the entry team leader.

Mike smiles through the pain. We got him, he thinks to himself. I got him.

A faint whistling noise echoes through the sky and treetops, and then there is a brilliant, blinding flash of light.

* * *

Dave and Amy dance to the song playing, echoing softly through the bunker.

DJ and Julia look at them and then smile awkwardly at each other, and they continue preparing the full course dinner. DJ puts down the spoon in his hand and begins staring at Julia, beside him. She sees him staring out of the corner of her eye. She glances at him for a brief second and then continues to empty some cans of vegetables. Her face begins to blush.

DJ grabs ahold of her hand, "Will you dance with me?"

Justin walks into the kitchen after returning from the restroom, and time seems to stand still as he looks at the scene before him. Memories of his wife begin flowing through his mind, and then the peaceful scene begins to slightly upset him, especially the somewhat intimate interaction between DJ and Julia. Justin scoffs at them and heads to the operations room to turn off the music.

Justin reaches for the music player and then stops, distracted by the static blur on several cameras of the CCTV monitors.

Then, a slight rumble vibrates throughout the entire bunker. The lights powered by the generator begin to flicker.

Everyone stops dancing after the small disturbance and Justin turns off the music.

Justin walks back to the kitchen to confirm what he saw and felt with the others. Before he can speak, another rumble rolls throughout the bunker.

Small clinking noises are heard, of things vibrating around.

They look at each other with fear, fear of the worse. Panic begins rushing through all of their faces.

"Kill the generators!" Justin says to Dave, as he was closest to the hallway.

"Brian!" Julia says, running towards his room.

A few minutes go by and they all link up in the dim operations room, now only being lit by battery powered lamps. They wait patiently as Justin scans through the video footage from around the cabin, before it went to static.

One flashlight from a headlamp appears on the CCTV footage from inside the cabin.

It was Robert.

The living room camera in the cabin could only pick up flashes of light coming from the kitchen area, clearly from Robert looking around and resupplying their rations.

Justin forwards the tape about ten minutes and then slows the footage. Dark outlines of other bodies and several flashlights jump around for a few seconds on the CCTV footage, and then the camera turns to static.

Amy gasps and covers her mouth. Dave hugs her and looks at Julia, frozen by the footage.

Justin pulls up camera footage from the perimeter of the cabin at the same time, and there is a brief flash of light in the skyline and then that footage turns to static too.

Julia shakes her head and wipes her face. She walks over to the corner of the room and pulls out an automatic rifle from their small arsenal, and then she begins loading a magazine. Then she starts loading extra ammunition and small explosives into a backpack.

They all stand silently and watch her.

Justin and DJ look at each other. Dave pulls Amy into the other room and DJ follows them, knowing there is nothing they can say to help, and it is not their place to.

"Julia," Justin says calmly as he walks over to her.

Julia ignores him and continues preparing, as if she is mounting an attack.

Justin grabs her firmly by the arms and stops her movement.

"Stop. Julia, stop." Justin says softly and pulls her tightly into his arms.

Julia struggles, and Justin holds her stronger. She stops resisting and then begins weeping into Justin's chest.

The faint muffled moans of Julia's sorrow are the only sounds that can be heard throughout the dark bunker, the bunker that is now hopelessly silent.

TWENTY-FIVE

Richard approaches the water fountain and sits beside Nichole and Li-Li.

"Alright, so let's make this quick and go over the numbers. Were there anymore from the last group you talked with?" He asks Nichole, and then begins looking at the notebook of drawings from Li-Li again.

"No. Six was all that I could get, not counting Lilly and myself."

"Okay. Well, I've got two more from the last group that I met with. They are a little older, but still in pretty good shape. I think they'll be able to make it, physically. So, that brings our total to nineteen. And that's counting all three of us as well."

Richard puts down the notebook and looks to Li-Li.

She takes a breath and then nods her head, yes.

Richard lets out a small sigh of relief that she is going with them and that she has not changed her mind, and he smiles.

"Great. So, the next thing we need to do is...hang on, my phone is vibrating like crazy." He reaches into his pocket for his phone.

Nichole and Li-Li's phones begin ringing at the same time.

The mass alert loudspeakers from around the base come on, "Please find access to a media source...Please find access to a media source."

They see the 'Breaking News' messages light up on their phones. They look at each other with uncertainty about what is going on.

Across the open pavilion and shopping area are numerous security guards and TSOMBIE employees from the community. They are all walking toward a large electronic billboard on top of a building. The billboard flashes red.

Richard, Nichole and Li-Li, all begin walking toward the billboard as well.

'Breaking News' banners scrolled across the screen with a large 'ANN' logo. Two reporters appear on the screen from behind a news anchor desk, with images of Robert Rawlings, Julia Rawlings, and Justin Brown, displayed in the corner of the screen.

"Thank you for viewing this Breaking News Alert. ANN has just received confirmation from government officials this morning that Robert Rawlings, Julia Rawlings, and Justin Brown, have all been killed during a government raid on their hideout, late last night. As you recall, these three fugitives were wanted for their connection with the attacks on AGI and government facilities earlier this year. The general population may now disregard all previous lookout and warning messages for these three individuals. Please tune in tonight for the full story with ·Ms. McNeil, and for our regularly scheduled news updates. Thank you for listening. Goodbye."

Richard begins walking away after the crowd disperses.

Nichole and Li-Li look at each other with shock, and full of emotions, and questions.

Richard makes it to a nearby bench just as his knees seem to give out and he almost collapses, bracing himself on the edge of the bench.

Nichole hurries over to him. "Rich, Richard." She says, grabbing ahold of his arm.

Richard doesn't respond. He just stands there, holding onto the bench and staring down at the ground.

Nichole looks back at Li-Li, and then at the CCTV camera nearby. She motions with her head for Li-Li to help her move Richard back to the water fountain. They help him up with one arm wrapped slightly around each of their shoulders, trying to appear as casual as possible.

"Come on, Richard. Walk to the fountain. You are going to draw attention to us helping you. We need to remain calm and act normal. And we need to talk about this and what it means for us." Nichole pleads.

They sit him down on the fountain and Richard looks up at them, full of rage. It is a look that they have never seen from him before.

"Talk? Talk about what, Nichole? It is over. Over. There's nothing left to talk about. Did you not just see that? It's over." Richard pushes away from them as he stands and walks off.

Nichole looks down and wipes her eyes. She feels sick to her stomach by the sudden rush of emotions. She takes a seat by the fountain. She knows that he is right.

Li-Li watches Richard walk away, and she turns to Nichole. She takes a seat on the fountain wall beside her. She too, feels weak from the sudden change in everything. Everything that they were planning. She is upset that she can longer help them. And she begins to think. She begins to think that she has made everything worse for them, because she gave them a false sense of hope. And that hope was now gone.

TWENTY-SIX

Muffled voices. Light, cloudy shades of blue. Cottonmouth. Numbness of limbs. Different beeping tones.

The crust cracks around Mike's eyelids as they begin to open, slowly and wider.

"Sweetie?" Mike hears his wife say. He sees Melissa's face leaning over him, a little distorted at first but it starts getting clear as his eyes continue adjusting. Then he feels her lips on his forehead. He begins to regain his sense of touch. He can feel the stiffness of the brace around his neck.

She begins to back away, but he grips her hand with the tips of his fingers before she pulls it away from the hospital bed.

"Closer." Mike whispers out and opens his eyes a little wider.

Melissa leans back in to kiss him again.

"They tried to…kill me." He manages to whisper out, close to her ear.

His strength gives out and he lets go of her hand.

Melissa pulls back slowly after he lets go and she wipes her eyes, confused and shocked at what he just said. She looks at the camera in the corner of the room and waits for Mike's eyes to turn and see it.

"Mike, you are at The Society headquarters hospital." She says, nodding her head to make sure he understands that they are being watched.

Mike closes and opens his eyes, signaling back to her that he understands.

A young doctor enters the room, with a small, touchscreen tablet in his hand. He looks at Melissa and smiles, and then he moves around the bed and stands beside Mike.

"Mr. Hardy. How do you feel, sir?"

"Betrayed," he mumbles softly under his breath.

"I'm sorry, sir? I couldn't quite hear you." The doctor waits a second and after no response, he looks at Melissa.

She shakes her head as if she didn't hear what Mike said either, but she did hear him.

Mike looks at her and she tilts her head slightly in the direction of the camera again.

Mike lets out a hard gush of air through his nostrils.

The doctor walks to behind the bed and raises the backrest, until Mike is sitting almost upright.

Mike lets out a few light groans from the shift in his body position. He looks at the chipper doctor and his light display of arrogance he has about him. He isn't a TSOMBIE, Mike thinks to himself.

"Well sir, the good news is that nothing appears to be permanent." The doctor says, looking down at his tablet and swiping the screen back and forth with his fingers a few times.

"Mild concussion and whiplash. Various lacerations. Soft tissue damage from the explosion. And several ligament tears in your left knee and ankle, as well as a hairline fracture. We are going to run a few more tests and change your bandages, but, you will be able to go home later today. And then you will continue your recovery with outpatient services. We will keep the braces on your neck and leg for three to four weeks. You will also be assigned a house medical team until you are completely healed. But like I said, nothing is permanent. I am sure that you will make a full recovery in no time at all. Any questions, sir? Ma'am?"

Mike and Melissa both look at him, and then at each other.

"Okay then. Well, sir, I would just like to personally thank you for what you did, for The

Society. And for all of the sacrifices that you and your family have made for us, for everyone."

The doctor puts his right hand over his heart for a few seconds, smiling at Mike.

Mike just stares at him, completely untouched by his words.

The doctor turns on the television as he exits the room.

Mike's father appears on the screen a few seconds later.

Mike growls softly to himself in anger, and Melissa moves to his side to comfort him and keep him calm.

"Mike, I wanted to tell you how proud I am of you, and to thank you for what you have done for The Society. I know you are in some pain right now, but I have talked with the medical staff there, and they have assured me that you will make a full recovery. And I also want you to rest assured in knowing that your sacrifice will be greatly rewarded. What I'm saying, Mike, is that you did it. You have proven yourself, to me, and to everyone within The Society, and therefore you have officially earned the title and role as my successor. Congratulations. Now, I am going to publicly announce your rightful position as my second in command as soon as you are back up and functioning. Tasha will remain in charge until that time and prepare everything for your transition. So, for the time being, get some rest. And contact me directly if you, or Melissa and the kids need anything, anything at all. Job well done, son! Melissa, take care of our hero!"

The television turns off.

Melissa stands beside Mike's bed and just looks at him, wondering what he is thinking. She wants to know why Mike said that to her, that they tried to kill him. But, she knows that it is not safe to talk about it there, especially if he was telling the truth.

Only one thing runs through Mike's mind as he stares into the mirror-like reflection of the blank television screen, looking at his handicapped body by the doing of his father and Tasha. Revenge.

TWENTY-SEVEN

Several days go by since Robert was killed.

The bunker was silent. Silent in grief. The only breaks in silence came from the pitter-patter of Samantha running around with her toys.

The generators were shut off after the explosion to eliminate all unnecessary noise that might draw attention to the bunker area.

The possibility of The Society finding the bunker had increased, but it was still very unlikely that they would ever find them. The bunker was over five miles away and deep underground, well concealed. And even though the thought of The Society finding them was at the back of everyone's mind, they were not scared.

Their leader had died. Without Robert, the thought of getting out of the bunker faded away, and the waiting game began. Not waiting to get out of the bunker like before, this was the waiting-to-die-slowly game. A game that they all knew from the very beginning they might have to play one day. And it seemed as if that day had now come.

Conversations in the bunker were now very brief and to the point, and none of their short talks ever included anything about what had happened.

DJ stays in the operations room most days and nights, fiddling around with the computers and continuing to decrypt files, just to keep himself occupied and to pass time.

Justin keeps to himself. He eats alone. He avoids playing his favorite handheld game to eliminate any chance of feeling excited about anything again, and for fear of destroying it out of anger. He exercises to the point of collapse to help himself sleep at night. There was no alcohol left to help with that anymore. No more resupply runs.

Dave and Amy keep to themselves, with Samantha. They say the occasional good morning or good night to DJ and Justin but that is about the extent of their interaction.

Brian's routine never changes. But it would likely never change due to his Phase Two condition. DJ takes on the responsibility of watching over him while Julia remains isolated in her room, avoiding contact with anyone.

Julia lies in bed, day and night, completely numb by the loss of her father. She stares into the dark emptiness of her room when her eyes are not closed. Everyone takes turns in trying to talk with her, but all attempts end unsuccessful with no response.   Amy brings her food and water every day, but Julia rarely touches it, only enough to stay alive it seems. Julia makes an occasional trip to the restroom every day and then returns straight back to her bed, never speaking, or even looking at anyone.

Loneliness and hopelessness were the only things that now filled the stale, cold bunker air.

TWENTY-EIGHT

"Tasha. Please, come in and have a seat." Mr. Hardy says from behind his new headquarters desk. "You said over the phone that you had a few updates since the full debrief on the operation. Is that correct?"

"Yes, sir." Tasha says, as she sits and open a folder. "We had three more forensic search teams fly in to the area, and we expanded the search to a one-mile radius around the cabin. There are no signs of anyone else or anything new, but we will continue to search and observe the area for a few more days, just in case. And, the DNA results finally came back on the two sets of bone fragments found on site, the bones not belonging to our agents or Robert Rawlings. The DNA results are ultimately inconclusive, but we are confident that they are the remains of Julia and Justin based on the other corresponding pieces of evidence."

"Inconclusive?"

"Yes, sir. The last two sets of bones were found in a state of previous decomposition, which made it harder to get accurate DNA results, especially after they were degraded even further by the explosion. Based on the decomposition analysis, we believe that after they died, they were then buried on the property by Robert Rawlings. And, the team only identified seeing Rawlings in the cabin before the airstrike. So, everything lines up with it being them. It is over, sir. We got them."

"Great work, Tasha. I am so glad that we can finally close the chapter on this one. I was almost beginning to think that it would never happen."

There is an awkward moment of silence as Mr. Hardy smiles at her, ingenuine.

"So, how close are your departments on being complete with the transition to our new headquarters here? We haven't discussed that in a while."

Tasha breathes out a small sigh of relief that he did not say something else that she though was coming.

"Sir, everyone, and all of our departments, will be relocated and fully operational by the end of this month. And there will be no gaps in coverage for our ongoing operations."

"By the end of this month? Before the monthly board meeting?"

"Yes sir, we are ahead of schedule."

"Great. We can hold the board meeting here then. This will be the perfect setting for the announcements to be made. Mike's accomplishment on finding Rawlings has undoubtedly swung all of the undecided votes in my, our, favor. And since everything did not go according to our Plan B, and Mike ended up surviving the blast, he is the next logical choice as my successor. I'm not even sure the board would consider anyone else at this point. We could never get rid of him now or keep him hidden from the limelight. I mean, he is pretty much a hero now. And, that is not necessarily a bad thing. For us, I mean."

Mr. Hardy stands from behind the desk and sits down beside Tasha on the sofa.

Tasha holds her breath and remains silent, knowing what is inevitably coming next.

"I have always been able to count on you, Tasha. And I know, that when the time comes, you will continue to do what is needed for us, to do what is best, for The Society."

Tasha fights back her emotions and struggles to remains calm and professional, even though it is crushing her with every breath she takes.

She nods quietly in understanding and breathes calmly.

"Excellent. I knew you would understand." Mr. Hardy stands and smiles, and then he walks back to his desk and takes a seat.

"Now then, I would like to discuss your future role in the organization, after Mike comes back."

"Yes, sir." She says with a slight tremble in her voice, after swallowing her pride and holding down her emotions.

"I found out that Mike was actually able to turn over some new stones in the bloodline camp. So, I am going to put you in charge of the camp. I will make the official announcement at the board meeting, along with Mike's new appointment. But in the meantime, I would like for you to go ahead and get a better feel for the dynamics within the camp, and then brief me with an updated plan for future reproduction purposes. Expand on what Mike already discovered down there through his interviews. I think this will be a great opportunity for you to stay relevant and remain popular within The Society, especially if you are able to locate any more contacts of Rawlings that we might not know about."

"Thank you, sir. I will do my best, as always. And what about the Phased injection plan for the Society bloodlines, sir? The ones that are not in the Inner Circle? Am I still…"

"There's no change with that, Tasha. Yes, you are still the lead for planning and implementation of their phased conversion into TSOMBIEs. We can meet later this week and discuss updates with those plans. I think we may even be able to speed up the timeline on their phased injections, with our recent advancements in the research and development labs. Follow up on that."

"Yes, sir. I'll look into it. And, thank you, sir."

Mr. Hardy smiles, and then logs into his computer and begins typing, signaling the meeting is now over.

Tasha gets up and leaves the office in silence. She feels a brewing animosity towards a man that could turn his back on someone, so quick and so cold.

What was I thinking? He was willing to kill his own son. So why should I expect him to feel any different about me? Tasha asks herself, staring at him one last time as she closes the door.

* * *

On the first floor of the new headquarters building, Walter Rockmann and General James shake hands and take a seat in Mr. Rockmann's new office.

"So, Trip, how does it look for you?"

"I don't have a single vote left, Walt. I would give them all to you if I did. I plan to announce my withdrawal to the board at the monthly meeting. And you? What does your support look like now that Hardy succeeded in getting rid of Rawlings?"

Mr. Rockmann pours a fresh drink for the two of them.

"Three. I have three confirmed votes left, Trip."

Mr. Rockmann takes a drink and lights a cigar, offering General James one. He accepts the cigar and then takes the lighter from Mr. Rockmann.

"But, I am going to concede and withdraw my name as well. There is no since in having anyone risk their reputations for nothing. Myself included."

The General exhales and raises his glass to Mr. Rockmann, "It was a refreshing thought while it lasted."

"Yes. Yes, it was."

Mr. Rockmann raises his glass back and they toast in unison, "The Society."

TWENTY-NINE

"Mike!" Melissa yells as she enters the bedroom and sees Mike standing at the foot of the bed.

She rushes over and eases him back onto the bed.

"Mike, come on. What are you doing? You know you shouldn't be putting any pressure on your leg yet."

Mike looks at her with pain in his eyes, his eyes that still have a few busted capillaries from the explosion. Then he lets out a sigh as he moves his neck around slightly, within the surrounding brace.

"What do you need, sweetie? I'll get it."

"My phone."

Melissa nods and retrieves his work phone from across the room.

"Not that phone."

She stares at him with curiosity for a moment. She goes into their closet and brings back his personal phone, that is not tracked.

She holds on tight as Mike grabs the phone. They stare at each other for a moment.

"Talk to me, Mike. Is this about what you told me in the hospital?"

"Yes."

She walks to the window and watches their children playing outside. She wipes her eyes and walks back over to Mike.

Mike holds her hand, "I'm going to protect us."

"How? How can you protect us from them?"

"Remember what I told you about true immunity?"

Melissa nods. "Yes. What are thinking of doing, Mike?"

"I am going to finally expose their darkest secrets, about permanent and temporary bloodline immunity, to all of the Society members. And not just the secrets of my father and Tasha, but all of the secrets of the Inner Circle bloodlines too. That is the only way that we have a chance of living any kind of life of our own, not controlled by them."

"But you need hard proof. What proof do you have? The general population of Society members will not go against the Inner Circle, not without hard evidence, Mike."

"I'm going to get the evidence."

"How?"

Mike stares at her for a few seconds and then looks at his phone. "By doing what I have been doing all of my life, Melissa. By doing what I am trained to do."

Mike smiles at her with confidence and wipes the mascara from her cheek. He unlocks the screen on his private phone and dials.

"Scott…Yeah, it's me. We need to talk in private. I need to ask you for one last favor."

THIRTY

"Li-Li! Li-Li! Can you draw with me? Please?" Kenton knocks on the front door and looks through the windows of Li-Li's house for any signs of movement.

Li-Li rolls over on her bed and closes her eyes, trying to block out the sound of Kenton's innocent voice at her door.

Nichole drinks coffee on her front porch with Brent, and they watch as young Kenton gives up and finally walks slowly back to his yard, with his dog by his side.

A black SUV pulls into Nichole's driveway and two Society agents get out. "Mr. Brent Phillips, we need you to come with us, sir."

Brent finishes his cup of coffee and stands. Nichole hugs him goodbye.

"Alright, wish me good luck." He says, walking down the steps.

Nichole waves to him as the SUV drives away.

Nichole refills her coffee and returns to her seat on the porch.

And that was how life went on in the bloodline camp. People were taken off by The Society, individually, for more interviews and more reproduction examinations. Sometimes they would come back the same day, sometimes after a few days, and sometimes not at all. While the thought of never coming back was always at the back of their minds when they left with the agents, they were not scared.

Hope of surviving and escaping quickly faded away, it faded away just as fast as it had entered the camp.

THIRTY-ONE

"Julia." A familiar but rare voice wakes Julia.

"Julia, I love you. I missed you."

"Brian?" Julia turns over and quickly sits up in her bed.

Brian leans over and hugs Julia softly.

Julia hugs him back tightly and looks at DJ standing in the doorway, smiling. She backs Brian up with her hands, taking another look at him. Her eyes water quickly and she hugs him again, closing her eyes and then tears begin rolling down her cheeks. She holds him for a long, emotional moment.

DJ clicks a small handheld recorder. "Hey, Brian, come here and shake my hand buddy."

Julia watches as Brian walks over to him and shakes his hand.

Justin enters the kitchen after exercising and observes what is happening, without being noticed by them.

DJ turns Brian around after they shake hands and they both look at Julia. DJ smiles at her astonished expression.

"How? How did…"

DJ tosses her the recording device.

"I've been playing around with the binaural coding for messages. It's just a basic frequency right now, so the messages can't be that complex. But after some more research, I think I will be able to create a more advanced frequency that will allow for more complex messages, possibly to the point of permanently changing his behavior pattern and actions, forever. I mean, it will take me some time to do it, but after what I have been able to do so far, well, I think that…"

Julia rushes to DJ from her bed and hugs him tight, and sincere.

DJ smiles and begins to blush a little.

Julia backs away and looks up at him, deep into his innocent and caring eyes.

There is something familiar in his eyes, in how he is looking at her. It has always been there, now that she thinks about it.

She moves her hand slowly behind his neck and pulls him close, until their noses gently touch. They both close their eyes and Julia kisses him with a soft, timeless kiss.

Justin looks on, still unnoticed by them. He thinks of his wife Claire, and the time they once shared together. And he smiles. He smiles for Julia, knowing how she feels in that moment. Complete. Full of love. Full of life. And full of hope.

THIRTY-TWO

Mike eases out of the passenger seat of his car and steadies himself with a walking cane. He looks back into the car before he shuts the door, his wife and two sons looking back at him.

"We will be right here waiting for you. Good luck, Mike."

"Yeah, good luck, Dad," his sons echo.

Mike smiles and makes his way inside the new Society headquarters building, along what used to be Pennsylvania Avenue.

Immediately after entering the front doors, Mike is escorted past security screening and straight to the new conference center.

"Please have a seat here, Mr. Hardy. Someone will come get you when they are ready for you inside."

Mike sits and watches the security guard post at the other end of the hallway. Mike looks around the hallway.

Pictures of his father and the Hardy Family lined the walls, along with other prominent, Inner Circle bloodlines.

He grinds his teeth at the decades of power and wealth along the walls, and he begins to second guess himself about going against all of them.

He looks down at his watch.

He is half an hour early.

Mike takes a deep breath and tries to calm his nerves as he continues to wait.

* * *

"Thank you for the kind words, Mr. Rockmann, and General James. I also want to thank everyone that was involved with the election process, and for all of the hard work that went into everyone's campaign efforts. Pending any objections from the board, we will make the official message broadcast next month to all Society members and the civilian population. I would like to give Mike just a little more time to heal. And speaking of my son, Mike."

Mr. Hardy stands and signals to the guard at the door.

The guard opens the door and motions to Mike, "They are ready for you inside, sir."

All of the board members in the large conference room stand, and they all begin to clap as Mike limps into the room, on his cane.

Mike sees Scott at the back of the conference room, near the computer control panel, and they make brief eye contact with each other, as Mike shakes his father's hand in front of everyone.

Tasha looks at who Mike is looking at. She sees Scott hold his thumb in the air and Mike nods.

She briefly wonders why, as the clapping lulls and everyone begins taking their seats.

"I asked Mike to be here today in person for this special occasion, for both myself and for him. So, without any further delay. By the authority vested in me, I officially appoint, Michael Hardy, Junior, as my successor, and second in command of The Society! Well deserved, son!"

Mr. Hardy shakes Mike's hand again.

Everyone claps in another large round of applause.

Mike grips his father's hand as hard as he can and utters sternly, "Have a seat, Dad."

Mr. Hardy looks at his hand coloration as Mike releases the grip and sits. He then looks at Mike and the crowd with an awkward smile from the exchange.

The clapping subsides and the room full of over eighty board members take their seats.

Most of the board members were physically present for the commencement of the new headquarters building. But there were a handful of Society board members on the teleconference monitors, still overseas, in different regions of the new America.

The room and screens grow silent, waiting for Mike to speak.

Mike looks out and into the room, and he takes a deep breath.

There it was, everything Mike had wanted, everything he had worked so hard for was now right in front of him. But as he looked around the room, images of his wife and his boys filled his mind now, not this, not The Society.

"You know, ever since I was just a boy, this was all I ever wanted to do. I looked up to my father, my grandfather. I respected them. I wanted to be them. I wanted to take over and lead The Society, as all my forefathers had done before me."

Mr. Hardy's tension eases by Mike's words.

"This was a rough year for us, especially for me. I never thought I had a chance of carrying on the Hardy legacy after my previous failures. Then, I found Rawlings. But I almost died in the process. And while I was lying on the ground in the woods that night, bleeding out, floating in and out of consciousness, our motto kept running through my mind. The motto of The Society, imagine the greatness people can achieve if someone forces their hand. That motto is an important part of our history. But history…well, history can be a funny thing. It is easy to manipulate history if certain details are left out."

Mike pauses and nods to Scott in the back of the room, "Now, please."

Everyone looks around, somewhat confused if they had heard him right.

Mike smiles and waits.

Then, within a matter of seconds, phones start vibrating and ringing around the room, with a mass alert message.

Mike looks at Tasha and his father and smiles.

"So, I would like to thank Ms. McNeil and my father, for forcing my hand to greatness."

The speakers in the conference room come on, and video clips of Tasha and Mr. Hardy talking appear on the large television screens.

"…And everything is set to start implementing TSOMBIE injections for all Society members not within the Inner Circle? Right after I give my election acceptance speech?"

"Yes, sir. We have confirmed all tests with the temporary immune vaccines that all Society members outside the Inner Circle have been injected with over the past century, and all of our test subjects have been successfully converted into TSOMBIEs…"

A large wave of gasps flows throughout the conference room from all Society members not within the Inner Circle. Yelling and screaming begins. And the Inner Circle members and Mr. Hardy start trying to convince the other members to calm down and that it is not true.

Mike smiles in thanks to Scott, and then begins limping out of the conference room, now filled with chaos. Mike continues limping down the hallway, smiling with each painful step.

"Security! Seal the conference room doors!" Mr. Alex Miller says, a senior Society member that was not in the Inner Circle. "By executive order one, one, seven, I hereby assume authority as the senior member of The Society. And I call a vote for immediate removal of all Inner Circle Society members, for reasons detrimental to the good order and future of the organization. All those in favor?"

All the board members, more than sixty that are not part of the Inner Circle, all raise their hands in favor.

"Guards!" Mr. Miller yells.

Five more guards enter the conference room.

"Secure all of the Inner Circle members and transport them to our secure holding facility immediately."

Mr. Miller looks around for Scott and finds him after a moment of scanning the room.

"Scott Barnes, right?"

"Yes, sir."

"Thank you for what you did. I saw you at the computers back there."

Scott shakes his hand.

"Watch over these clowns for a minute. I need to talk to Mike before he leaves the building."

Scott nods and watches the older gentleman run slowly out of the conference room and down the hall.

"Mike! Hey, Mike! Wait a second!"

Mike presses the hold button on the elevator doors before they close.

"Mr. Miller."

They look at each other and Mike takes a deep breath, not fully knowing what he is going to say. Then, Mike looks down at Mr. Miller's hand, extended for him to shake. Mike lets out his breath and shakes his hand.

"Mike, based on what you did in there, you should still be placed in charge. And well, I know the other members like me, that are not in the Inner Circle, feel the same way, that we can trust you to lead us. We need someone like you, someone that has the courage and integrity to help fix this mess."

Mike looks at Mr. Miller for a moment and thinks briefly about what he was asking of him.

"I'm sorry, but I just don't want that life anymore. And I am sure that you will do just fine, Mr. Miller. The Society has been long overdue for some 'real' change. I have to go now."

Mike pulls his hand back and releases the hold button on the elevator doors.

They smile at each other and Mr. Miller knows he will never see him again.

The doors begin closing and Mike finishes his parting words, "The life I want is outside, and they are waiting for me."

Thank You

*I would personally like to thank you for
reading American Z - Bloodlinez.*

*And most of all,
and most importantly,
I hope you enjoyed it.*

*Sincerely,
J.G. Fletcher*

About the Author

J.G. Fletcher is a self-published, American author of fiction. He is a resident of Clarksville, TN and alumnus of Austin Peay State University, TN. He graduated with honors from APSU, with a BS in Criminal Justice/Homeland Security and a MS in Management.

J.G. Fletcher has also been serving proudly in the Armed Forces since 2001. He is a Veteran of Operation Iraqi Freedom and Operation Enduring Freedom.

Other Published Works

American Z

TSOMBIE

Join the TSOMBIE Program today and receive your Phase Three Message Package, which includes newsletters and promotional discounts. More information about this and the author, including current and future works, can be found on the official author websites listed below.

Official Website:
https://jg-fletcher.com   or   https://tsombie.com

Facebook Page:
https://www.facebook.com/AmericanZOfficialBook

Author Email:
jg-fletcher@jg-fletcher.com